ONLY DISCONNECT

Third Flatiron Anthologies
Volume 4, Summer 2015

Edited by Juliana Rew
Cover Art by Keely Rew

Only Disconnect
Third Flatiron Anthologies
Volume 4, Summer 2015

Published by Third Flatiron Publishing
Juliana Rew, Editor

Discover other titles by Third Flatiron:
(1) Over the Brink: Tales of Environmental Disaster

(2) A High Shrill Thump: War Stories

(3) Origins: Colliding Causalities

(4) Universe Horribilis

(5) Playing with Fire

(6) Lost Worlds, Retraced

(7) Redshifted: Martian Stories

(8) Astronomical Odds

(9) Master Minds

(10) Abbreviated Epics

(11) The Time It Happened

License Notes

www.thirdflatiron.com

Contents

*****~~~~****

Editor's Note

by Juliana Rew

This edition calls upon Presentism as a theme: the pitfalls of distraction, overstimulation, and other attention thieves—too much to do, too little time. We asked: Are we becoming ADD? What are the advantages of being "in the present," or even bored?

We open with Evan Henry's near-future detective thriller set in Shanghai, "Seventh Sense," a world where there are "too many people" and the State tightly monitors everyone. What would you do to have just three minutes to yourself?

Arrest and interrogation with undisclosed charges is a common science fiction nightmare, but Steve Coate adds a new twist in his dark tale, "Jacked." ("But officer, I wasn't even there, I tell you.")

We're so connected to our identity as human beings, it's interesting to contemplate what would happen if we had to take an alien perspective into account, as in Jonathan Shipley's "Aqua Equal," a fun tale about the first Earth student to attend college with our alien overlords. Evelyn Deshane takes us to the "Carnival of Colours," where aliens judge you by the color of your name.

We're featuring a lot of game-related excitement in this issue. Stephanie Flood's Adventure-style yarn, "A House of Mirrors," and Jason Lairamore's "She Dies," show us that it's not always "just a game," but that's the fun of it, right?

Though it saves us the trouble of dating, online romance can be risky, and it's even more so if the intelligent AI running the network doesn't like mushy stuff, as in E. E. King's "Just Visulate."

We can't resist a bit of the steampunk, of course. In Matt Weinburg's "The Eyes in the Water," a young

7

blogger gains a wide audience as he tracks the mystery of his deceased uncle's intelligent creation.

Connect with the Earth rather than Bluetooth? Maybe going back to Nature is the solution to today's over-booked world. When a couple goes camping together in Adria Laycraft's "Killing the Green Man," we learn that's not always the case.

It's just a gut feeling, but we think Robert Lowell Russell is onto something when he says "Super Bugs" are about to give us a nudge.

Other humorous offerings for this round include Elliotte Rusty Harold's "Email Recovered from Genetech Debris, Lieutenant Jeffrey Abramowitz Investigating" and Wendy Nikel's "Life After Download." Whew, take a breath. And then call your mother.

Finally, we close with Paul Barclay's luminous "Into the Light," where we learn that even though you can't hug a hologram, even a character who's not very likable or connected with people can still have the best of intentions that turn out to benefit humanity.

"Only Disconnect" proudly showcases an international group of new and established speculative fiction authors, who help us decide whether it's time to disconnect—or instead to connect even further.

*****~~~~~*****

Seventh Sense

by Evan Henry

Li Chen maneuvered his bicycle around the sharp right turn onto rain-slick Chiang Street at rush hour, his legs alternately rising and falling on the pedals of the old ten-speed. He had cut through the financial district of Lujiazui, beneath the glittering towers of the international banks, past the luxurious hotels and four-star restaurants populated by oilmen, commodities traders, and their wives. He was nearing the western end of Shanghai now, far from the city's port and perhaps three kilometers from his customer's home in a posh inland villa on an artificial hillside.

Tucked safely away inside his jacket's inner pocket was a small plastic bag holding twenty-four tablets of Solus, a two-week supply for all but the heaviest users. This, like perhaps a quarter of all the Solus in Shanghai, was Li Chen's own product, but right now his problem was that he had not taken a dose himself in nearly fifteen hours.

There had been a bust about a week ago, the federal police descending on two of his safehouse locations along the southern fringe of the city, taking with them exactly half of his ten-man crew. He shuddered to think where they might be now. He had barely slept in the past three days, having taken it upon himself to complete all the necessary deliveries to the far western regions personally. With the danger he asked his men to place themselves in, he felt it a matter of honor. With that honor, though, came an unavoidable degree of danger, one that necessitated regular consumption of Solus to keep one's absence from the all-encompassing Syncom network uninterrupted. Li, though, had been less than fully diligent about his own intake.

He swerved to avoid an elderly woman who had stepped out into the bike lane. His sleep-deprived brain was slipping, and what was worse, the familiar blue glow of the network display was beginning to creep back into his peripheral vision. His 3A interface was slowly coming back online, and if he didn't take a dose of Solus soon, his uplink to the Syncom net would be complete, and his capture by the Shanghai police, or even the imperial authorities themselves, would be all but assured.

It was a drug with a user base as wide as it was diverse, totaling perhaps ten million and encompassing people of every ethnic group and social class. Disrupt the Solus supply for three days, and everyone living off the net, every democratic dissident or anti-corporate reformer, every government whistleblower, and, yes, every two-bit opium dealer would have their cover blown, and the labor camps out west would need to make a lot of room. *And the communists, too,* Li thought. The irony in that notion could scarcely escape anyone with even the most basic knowledge of history. *And let ten million flowers bloom.*

At the other end of the spectrum, his clientele extended even to the wealthy upper crust of Shanghai industry, aging businessmen and women who still spoke the old, pure form of Mandarin in active resistance to the hybrid dialect that had come to dominate business and government in the imperial cities, the vernacular known to progressive champions and nationalistic detractors alike as MandarEng. People like them were entrenched enough in the corporate-imperial civil service that their intermittent absences from the net could be overlooked for the small cost of a well-placed campaign donation or a job offer to the right bureaucrat's ambitious young son.

But for its serious users, Solus had become far more than an occasional escape. Those without the means to bribe officials into looking the other way were forced to great lengths in an effort to escape detection, taking themselves as far out of the range of the Syncom 11G cell towers as possible. Many of them had gone south and west into the hill country, and beyond that to caves and deserted grottos in the dense mountain ranges. There were places deep within the valleys of Zhejiang province where a man could hide for a thousand years.

The thought of going to live with them had occurred to Li many times, to go toward the setting sun and vanish finally from the omnipresent net and all the soul-poison and self-centeredness it represented. But to flee was not for him. Li Chen may have fit the stereotype, a young idealist with radical notions and still more radical friends, but whatever ideals he held were easily trumped by more practical considerations.

People going off the net was commonplace—mechanical failures had been common in the early days of the chip; deaths happened all the time, and in rural areas that might conceivably result in someone "blinking off" the grid and not being reported missing for weeks or even months. The number of people leaving the grid could easily be analyzed and their names just as easily collected, but cross-referencing those occurrences with missing persons reports, death certificates, and perhaps nonexistent records of chips genuinely failing was much more difficult. Cases that were suspicious enough to get you watchlisted were those that resulted in you disappearing from the net for a very short time—twelve hours might indicate a novice trying a first dose of Solus and not following up in time to avoid detection—or those that occurred in high-population–density areas without any subsequent record of death or reports that the individual had gone missing.

Li Chen knew that he easily fit into this second category. He had been eighteen when he had taken his first dose, a runner for the west side kingpin Gayo Park, an undocumented Korean immigrant who did not officially exist inside China, and thus had managed to remain free of the Syncom implants. Park himself gave Li his first Solus, a white tablet so small and seemingly innocuous that he could never have believed that it would exert an unbreakable stranglehold on him for the rest of his life, where missing a dose would mean not the unpleasant detox effects endured by withdrawing opium addicts, but life imprisonment at best, and prompt execution at worst.

The blue glow at the edge of his vision became brighter, but Li Chen continued to pedal. It was only another two kilometers, and another four back to the safehouse. He would be fine.

...

"There are too many people in the world," Detective Yu Zhang told his partner, who sat beside him in the passenger seat of the new Nissan patrol car. "Yes, far too many people. Understand that, and the Solus problem explains itself. Nowhere to be alone, nowhere to simply think, no quiet, so few resources for everyone. And there are too few of the dutifully unmarried like me, so the problem can only get worse."

He leafed through the inch-thick stack of papers on his lap, equal parts security measure against the hackers they tracked and antiquated relic of the Shanghai police force of the twentieth century. "It's the whole package of overpopulation that people grow to fear. Even the wealthy have to see the hunger in the southern provinces. After the Restoration, those who could afford to eat became complacent, but it was only a matter of time before the rioters stopped blaming the emperor and started blaming those who had come out on top. Naturally, they want an escape—the rich, the poor, everyone—and Solus is there. It is their escape from too many others."

He selected one of the photos at random and pulled it out. "Take this lady, for instance." He tapped the color photograph. It was a woman, no older than twenty-five, with bright eyes and a wide smile. "Three years into a university education; computer science student—

12

computer science, my friend. Tell me she didn't have a future in a world like this. These aren't Luddites, Xiao. They're ordinary people, every bit as normal as you or me. But they're lost people." He ran his tongue over dry lips, muttered, "Desperate people."

Zhang looked out his rain-streaked window at the city streets beyond. At the opposite side of the street was an open-air market, teeming masses pouring in under the scattered tarps to take shelter from the falling torrents, becoming targets of resentful scowls from small-time grocers. Beside him, Xiao cleared his throat awkwardly. "I don't think that's it, sir," he said.

"What's that?" Zhang asked. He thought he had heard, but his partner had said it too quietly for him to be sure. He turned to look at the younger man. The lieutenant was visibly uncomfortable, his collar buttoned to the top in a way only the greenest of rookies did. He was trying to contradict the detective, but as respectfully as possible.

"I said, I don't think that's it, sir," Xiao said, speaking a bit louder now. "Two-point-one-billion may be too much for China to sustain for much longer, yes, but there is enough room worldwide to keep population density at a reasonable average. And there are certainly enough resources. It's simply a matter of how those resources are distributed. More food goes to waste in this country alone than. . . "

Xiao trailed off as Zhang began to chuckle. "Keep talking like a communist," the detective said, returning his attention to the papers laid out on his lap, "and you'll be lucky to keep your rank another two weeks. I'm not going to have to tell them you're a party member, am I?" He bookended the question with another chuckle.

"No, sir," Xiao said, suddenly serious. "I'm sorry, sir. I didn't mean to—"

"You need not apologize to me," Zhang said, locking his mouth into a rock-hard, too-solemn expression. "I'm sure a brief word of explanation to our

13

friends in the Conformance Committee will be more than enough to allay any concerns." He looked up at the lieutenant again, this time wearing a wicked grin.

"Sir, I didn't mean—" Xiao swallowed nervously, his deferential attitude now reduced to one of absolute terror. "That is, I only meant that—"

"Relax," Zhang said, and chuckled again. He slapped the lieutenant playfully on the arm. "That was a joke. You're free to express your opinions as you like, within reason. You don't tell anyone about my little friend—" He patted the place in his coat pocket where he had concealed a small flask of rice wine. "—and I don't tell anyone you're a communist. Deal?"

"Deal, sir," Xiao said, slowly regaining his composure. A smile threatened to peek through at the corners of his mouth. "But I want you to know that I'm not a communist. Really I'm n—"

"And I don't care," said Zhang, beaming with a wide, toothy grin. "We'll drink to our deal. How does that sound?" He produced the flask from his coat pocket and took a robust swig of the volatile liquid, passing it next to his partner. Xiao nodded politely and drank down a small mouthful, his eyes blinking and watering noticeably at its strength. He handed the flask back to Zhang.

"Strange as it may seem," the detective said as he put the flask back in his pocket, "with everything they taught you at the Academy about towing the party line and shining your shoes and keeping every stray hair in order, you are among friends in this force." Abruptly, he reached up and tousled Xiao's hair, eliciting a flinch from the lieutenant. "And the hair's not half as important as they told you. What's important is *this*." He tapped the badge at his chest, above the pocket that held his secret flask. "This tells everyone who we are, and what we do. This is what lets us bring order to the people who need it."

"Yes, sir," was all Xiao could think to say.

14

"The *too many* people who need it," said Zhang. "And what *you* need, Xiao, is to loosen up."

A light blinked from the steering yoke. He turned in its direction, and a bright yellow display filled his vision, melding into green where it overlapped the dreary grey-blue of the late afternoon sky above Shanghai. It was a map of the city streets, their position marked with a pink dot at its center. Less than two kilometers away, a blinking red dot denoted their newest objective. It was a dealer, one of the targets of their operation, moving northward along Chiang Street at a steady twenty kilometers per hour. His chip had switched back onto the Syncom network. Li Chen had missed a dose.

"Just not too loose," Zhang said. "Looks like we've got one on the move."

...

A light snapped on above him. He tried to move but could not. Li Chen had been drugged, and not with Solus.

"You are in an interrogation center." The voice came loud and boomed from somewhere in the blackness out of the path of the light's beam. "You are still in the city of Shanghai; that much I am legally obligated to tell you."

He knew that he was naked. Li tried to hold his head up straight, but his muscles were too weak, drowned beneath a wave of fatigue by whatever drug they had given him. He cursed himself for the mistake. He could have easily taken one of the customer's tablets for himself. Surely the customer would have understood, and may have even appreciated the precaution. Now Li had been busted, and his customer was certainly in danger.

"Today, Mister Li Chen," the voice said. "Today, we are going to have a conversation, you and I." Finally the voice's source stepped into view. The man was middle aged and unmistakably a policeman, wearing the casual, almost innocuous black business suits favored by the

15

detectives of the contraband task force of the federal secret police, the division tasked with disrupting the production and distribution of Solus. He was around six feet tall and nearly as wide, a hulking giant of a man. His face bore a strong chin and narrow cheekbones, his eyes a mottled not-quite-brown that suggested the mingling of Han and European blood. A handgun of the police force's favorite nine-millimeter variety was holstered at the man's hip.

"How pleasant that conversation will be," said the detective, "is up to you. Its content, unfortunately, is not." From somewhere in the darkness he produced a chair like that in which Li now sat. He leaned on the chair, but did not sit down. "Today you are going to tell me all about your Solus operation. As far as you are able to remember, you are going to tell us the names of your suppliers, the names of your clients, their addresses, their mothers' maiden names, the names of their favorite whores—everything."

Li Chen looked up into the detective's face, glaring and malicious. "I don't speak MandarEng," he said haltingly, trying to affect the coarse voiced consonants and rough, guttural vowels of the nearly extinct Wu topolect. It was an old strategy, one he had learned from his accomplices among the pickpockets and street fighters of old Beijing, to stall for time while an officer fluent in the speech of old Shanghai could be called in, hoping they would lose interest in the meantime. It had worked when he was a child, before the chip had been made mandatory, but now they certainly had full access to his file. They would know that he was a Beijing native, and surely as proficient in MandarEng as anyone of his generation; more importantly, they clearly knew already who he was—Li Chen, self-made master of the Shanghai Solus trade. It would not work, and even if it did, it would only delay the inevitable. He was well and truly finished now.

16

The cop slapped him with full force and leaned down to look him in the eye. Li's hair hung down around his face, partially obscuring his view of the detective.

"You are a native of Beijing and a known associate of the Transpacific Cartel," said the detective. He spoke slowly, in a tone mocking Li's attempt at inarticulate speech: "You speak MandarEng."

A surge of fear and adrenaline rushed through Li. He lifted his head and shook the hair from his eyes.

"Now, the first thing you are going to tell me about is your childhood."

…

That question took the prisoner aback, as it always did. It was the first step of the disorientation-and-recall process, meant to take the subject by surprise and thus loosen up any intentionally blocked memories. Start at the beginning, and, the theory went, the subject's recollection naturally would progress to the present, touching on everything in between in a handful of milliseconds. It was not properly understood as a process of remembering, but as what might be more aptly—and more philosophically—called *anamnesis*: a loss of forgetting; and it was the natural prerequisite for what was to follow.

The process of duplicating a human cortex was easily the most closely guarded secret of the nation's police force, but secrecy in a nation of over two billion people was of necessity a relative matter. In recent months some subjects had shown signs of conditioning intended to disrupt the process, anti-mnemonic cues that would dominate their mental focus with an irrelevant image or musical passage. Nonetheless, it was still the greatest technological advancement law enforcement had seen in years. After years of work, the fears of the conspiracy theorists and the radicals that the chip could be used to look through another human being's eyes had been realized, if only by means of a difficult and costly postmortem process. Many years ago, it had been a

17

proverb that one's life flashed before the mind's eye in the instant before death, and the entire operation hinged on that being true, but experience had shown that this life recall often needed some assistance.

"Your parents, Li Chen—they were wealthy, yes?" His recall of the details was sketchy, but he remembered enough to jog further memories in the subject. "Your mother was a musician, your father a businessman. Before you were born—before the Imperial Restoration, that is. The new empire, that was what really upset things, put you and your mother to work as menial laborers, factory workers. And I guess that would explain it, wouldn't it? Your antagonism towards the empire, towards order?"

Li Chen looked up at him without speaking, bruises beginning to show themselves where the detective had struck him.

"And Solus—well, it was only logical. When you couldn't make ends meet in the factories, you turned to trafficking opium. That was bad enough, but Solus, my friend? That was your worst mistake."

He looked the subject, the bound criminal known as Li Chen, in the eye for the first time. Here was a man who had been convicted and condemned to death already, and surely he knew that. However, Zhang saw in him none of the fiery idealism he had been told about, the fervor and lunacy that was said to characterize Solus users and, so much more, dealers. There was none of the passionate resolve that was to be found in the eyes of communist radicals or disgruntled would-be revolutionaries. Instead, as he had already seen in the eyes of so many, there was only fear, and a trace of that anger that always follows the realization that there is no longer any hope. Li Chen was lost, and he was desperate. Almost reluctantly, Zhang moved his hand to the holster at his side, waiting on the signal from Xiao that the process had been completed, that the man's cortex had been duplicated and filed away in the evidence sector of their subterranean data annex.

"Go to hell," the prisoner said finally, not in halting speech or fumbled pronunciations this time, but in clear, fluent MandarEng.

"Sir?" the voice was Xiao's; it came from the direction of the room's only door, unsure and trembling. Zhang's head snapped around to see his partner's head thrust, modestly but obtrusively, into the darkened room. "His cortex has been cleared. We have what we need, Detective."

"You don't open the door to tell me, Xiao," Zhang shouted. He pointed the gun immediately toward Li Chen, and, with hardly any attention to aim, pulled the trigger. He was closer when firing than protocol strictly demanded, and blood spatter from the man's head stained the front of his blue shirt. He holstered his pistol and turned toward his partner.

"Look, in a single interrogation, it doesn't really matter, but if you stick your head into a room with an ongoing multiple just to tell me about one out of four or five subjects—that's a problem. You break my concentration and theirs; you make it harder to collect the data."

He advanced toward Xiao, who now practically cowered in the doorway to the back room, his eyes wide in shame and worry. He tried to speak, but the words stumbled over one another. He managed to extend a hand, clutching a single white handkerchief. Zhang accepted it and began to swab the bright red blood from his shirt.

"When a cortex has been collated and copied, you send word through this." He tapped at the earpiece in his own ear, then gestured in the direction of the desk that lay on the other side of the room's two-way mirror. "What did you think the microphone was for?"

"I'm sorry, sir," Xiao finally managed to stammer. "I should have known. I read the interrogation manual in full, but. . . I broke protocol and. . . I—I will inform the Committee myself, sir. It won't happen again, b-but I ought to be disciplined."

Zhang tossed the handkerchief into a corner of the room to await the cleanup crew. "That won't be necessary, Xiao," he said, not quite managing to hide the twinge of annoyance in his voice. "Just don't let it happen again."

Xiao preceded the detective through the door, another breach of decorum but not an issue either of them felt the need to raise. Zhang stopped in the doorway to look back once more at the deceased Li Chen, now granted in death the final escape from the net that he had so ardently pursued in life. It was bitterly ironic. Once, he would have smiled.

"It's done now, anyway," he said.

...

Detective Yu Zhang stood alone in the barren kitchen of his one-room ground-floor apartment on the west end of Shanghai, near the industrial districts. His eyes were fixed out the apartment's sole window, above the sink, surveying the low rooftops and blue, soot-stained air of the early morning city. Beyond the tops of factories and warehouses, he could see the smokestacks, belching their thick gray clouds into the affronted air. On the counter in front of him was a single plastic bag containing twenty-four tablets of Solus, enough for two weeks. A feeling of loneliness cut through him suddenly, and paradoxically one of excessive connectedness. It was a pang of doubt, one he had first felt perhaps ten years ago, shortly after the chip had been made mandatory.

He allowed the pang of doubt to grow within him like roots spreading outward from his heart. The Conformance Committee would consider it grounds for dismissal, maybe even for termination. Strangely, he felt only pride at this realization. The sky grew brighter on the other side of the window, and his hope did, too. He smiled to think of what Xiao might say—or might refuse to let himself say—if he had known. Memories of crimes for which he could never hope to atone played at the edge of his awareness, but the thrust of his mind remained forward. Around him he could feel children that never were, and children that might be.

He pulled open the zip-seal of the thin plastic bag and reached inside, selecting at random one of the twenty-four white tablets; it made no difference which he chose. He raised it to his lips and, after the briefest moment of hesitation, swallowed it with his saliva. It would take twenty minutes, maybe less, for the drug to take effect, for the blue glow of the chip display to fade slowly from sight. One hour in, the long-range proximity sensor would blink off the display screens at TwentyOneSeven corporate headquarters, and the name Yu Zhang would become one of thousands on the Solus watchlist. It would take longer, at least two days, for him to become a wanted man, after someone in the police bureaucracy made the connection between his absence from work and his absence from the grid.

Closing the bag of pills and slipping it into his shirt pocket, Zhang turned to the front door. The police-issue backpack he had been given upon graduation from Academy, faded and tattered with years of use, sat just in front of the threshold. In it were a few changes of clothes, three days' worth of survival rations, a water bottle, a tent, a hunting knife. And a picture of his parents, the only family he had ever known. He picked the backpack up and slung it across one shoulder, then the other, grabbing the key to his apartment from the counter as he did so. The computers, phones, and other electronic artifacts of his life would remain behind, their significance now defunct. Even under the most thorough of analyses, he was confident they would reveal nothing but the ideal image of a good and obedient officer. Once, and not too long ago, he had been as straight-laced as they had come.

Zhang pulled the door open and felt the familiar blast of chill mid-autumn air. The dark sky was cloudless in the west, but high-altitude pollution obscured all but the brightest stars, the ones whose names he and the other children of his generation had never learned.

"There are too many people in the world," the detective muttered to himself as he twisted the key to lock his apartment door for the last time. He turned and looked east, where the dark blue of predawn had begun to turn a pale orange near the horizon. To the west, past the factories and far outside Suzhou, were hills and, in the distance, mountains upon snow-capped mountains. Beyond them were caves and deserted grottos, where a man could hide for a thousand years. He tossed the key into the shrubs abutting his kitchen window.

"Yes, too many people."

###

About the Author

This is Evan Henry's second appearance in a Third Flatiron anthology (previously in "The Time It Happened.") He is a writer, freelance editor, and one-man boon to the coffee industry. Though he is the editor in chief of Black Ship Books, a small UK-based publisher of comics and genre fiction, he claims to be severely underqualified, and is currently pursuing a BA in English. After reading the rest of the stories in this collection, you can check out more of his work at: BlackShipBooks.com

*****~~~~~*****

Super Bugs

by Robert Lowell Russell

Consciousness for us started with a mystery-meat burrito and a North Korean microwave. Trillions of us bacteria spent our days floating around in Dave's bowels. There wasn't much to do. When Dave fed us the kind of foods we liked, we made farts and sent him happy signals through his vagus nerve, which stretched all the way from his butt to his brain. When Dave fed us junk, as he usually did, we sent him little pangs of sadness instead. We weren't exactly controlling Dave, just nudging his mood a bit.

Eventually a few hundred million of us got bored with all the floating and nudging, and decided to tap into the vagus to see what was going on in Dave's mind. It was hard to decipher anything at first. Compared to the central nervous system, there's only a fraction of the neurons in the enteric nervous system. But when those first few hundred million of us learned to start sharing and comparing information, the jumbled sensory input resolved into the reality show that was Dave's life. The problem was, Dave never seemed to do anything interesting, and there was no way to change the channel.

One night while we were peeking in Dave's head, there was a news report about *super bugs,* and we got interested real fast. The story wasn't about the kind of bugs that crawled around Dave's apartment, pooping in his food. Super bugs were *microbes*, same as us, but they weren't like the caped crusaders we'd come to admire from Dave's comic books. Far from it. The super bugs were more like super *villains*, wreaking havoc on the human world. Confused but intrigued, we decided we needed more information.

23

The next time Dave went online looking for masturbation material, we sent him nudges until he clicked on a Wiki link about microbes. We didn't see much about super bugs, but we did see something about *Toxoplasma gondii*, a single-celled microbe that made mice wig out and attack cats. By that point, we weren't just intrigued, we were excited. Altering moods was one thing; turning mice into suicidal anti-cat commandos was a whole other ball game.

We decided to test what we could make Dave do. We waited until Dave was asleep and dreaming, because we figured our nudges would be more effective with fewer distractions—plus Dave was a sleepwalker. It also helped that Dave was nowhere near as complex as a mouse. As best we could tell, Dave was only motivated by fear and lust.

Manipulating Dave's lust was easy enough. Whenever Dave's dream thoughts flashed to breasts, we gave him happy nudges. Soon enough we got a physical reaction, but filling Dave's penis with blood was kind of lame.

Manipulating Dave's fears proved trickier. First we tried giving Dave sad nudges for dreamed images of clowns. Nothing. Then we tried spiders. Still nothing. After several more failures, a hundred million of us—the jokers mostly—suggested nudging images of bubbles. And that's when Dave's brain lit up like a Christmas tree.

Like most of Dave's thoughts, the repressed memory included boobs. Little Davey was hiding in his father's garage with a women's underwear catalog. Little Davey had his hand in his pants when Dave's dad came storming in.

"David, you're a filthy little boy!" shouted Dave's dad. "Filthy little boys get the Scrubbing Bubbles." Dave's dad squirted something from a spray bottle—we're pretty sure it was just dish soap and water—but as bubbles swirled around little Davey's head, all Davey saw were the cartoon images of S. C. Johnson's *Scrubbing Bubbles*®.

"They're eating me!" screamed little Davey. "Get 'em off me!"

More asleep than awake, grown up Dave's eyes shot open, and he bolted upright in bed. We could see his bedroom, but we could also see the dream images of those anthropomorphic, bristly bubbles superimposed in his vision. Dave flailed his arms, trying to shoo the bubbles away.

"Daddy!" he shrieked. "Make the bubbles stop! I'll be a good boy!" After a few more seconds of incoherent screaming, Dave collapsed back into his bed and resumed snoring.

We'd now learned by using our nudges that we could either engorge Dave's penis or get him to shriek and flail his arms. After a little practice, we managed to do both at once. We had to admit, getting Dave to freak out about bubbles was pretty funny, but it really wasn't what we'd hoped for. It seemed our experiment was a bust. Then Dave's foot fungus spoke up.

Normally we prokaryotes didn't mingle with eukaryotes. They've got their world, we've got ours, plus plenty of us were still pissed about that whole penicillin, antibiotics thing—bullshit that was an accidental discovery. Anyway, Dave's athlete's foot fungi noticed what we were up to and sent us a message through Dave's nervous system.

"Watch what we can do," they said.

Flipping their itching and burning settings to *high*, those fungi got one of Dave's feet to twitch. Then they did the same thing with the other foot. In bed, Dave responded by tossing and turning, and it dawned on us what the fungi had in mind.

It took several tries, but with our combined bubble terror flailing and the fungi's itchy feet burning, we managed to roll Dave out of his bed and onto his feet. His subconscious cerebellum kept him standing. With an itch, twitch, step on the left, and an itch, twitch, step, on the right, we got Dave shuffling around his dingy little apartment, while he shrieked, flailed, and sported a hard-on.

Then the few hundred million of us running the experiment were joined by *trillions* of other microbes who all of a sudden wanted in on the action. Offers of help came from bacteria colonies all throughout Dave's body. Not to be outdone, Dave's ringworm infection and other assorted yeasts and fungi offered to pitch in, too.

With a little arm flailing, hand clenching, and wrist twitching, we microbes managed to coordinate opening Dave's front door. Then we shrieked, shuffled, and flailed our way into the night.

Dave's first-floor apartment opened onto a street filled with bars and nightclubs in the college town he'd never left. The air smelled of fresh pizza, stale beer, and vomit. Bright lights beckoned. Music pounded from open doors.

Drunken humans staggered around us, whooping and pumping their arms in the air. With all our shrieking and flailing, we fit right in. Now and then, Dave threatened to wake from his somnambulism, but we just sent him deeper into Naked Lady Land, an invention of his own dreaming mind.

As we shuffled along, we learned to associate certain nerve impulses with corresponding motions. Our gait grew smoother and more confident. A subconscious thought from Dave told us the loud music places had sex inside. Dave was always obsessing about sex, so we lurched into one of the clubs to see what all the fuss was about.

Nearby, a woman with a strip of fungus growing on her lip danced bare-chested. Her breasts looked oddly flat and firm, but she had plenty of curves, particularly on her rippling arms. When we moved closer, the woman made her breasts twitch for us.

"Daddy!" we yelled over the music, "Make the bubbles stop! I'll be a good boy!"

"Not the worst pickup line I've ever heard," said the woman in a gruff voice.

...

The next morning, Dave woke up alone in bed happy, if a little sore. We microbes realized our error, of course, and resolved to work on recognizing gender cues, but overall we hadn't been impressed with sex. We *had* been impressed with Mustache Man's bulging arms and muscular chest, which were so much like the heroes in Dave's comic books. Looking Dave over as he stood in front of the bathroom mirror, we knew we'd have to do something about his flaccid body. And we'd need a cape.

...

Phase one of Operation Make Dave Awesome involved taking him to an all-night gym. He spent his nights dreaming in Naked Lady Land, while we pumped iron and practiced speaking. We encouraged Dave's adherence to a proper diet with happy nudges and diarrhea. We also knew a superhero needed good hair, so a particularly fluffy fungus volunteered to fill in Dave's bald spots.

When we discovered new colonies of bacteria growing after our Mustache Man encounter, a trillion of us went and wiped them out. No way were we sharing Dave's body with any more bugs. Antibodies from Dave's immune system were so impressed with our work that they let us take over defensive operations, freeing up more time for them to fix all the other things that were wrong with Dave.

Phase one took about four months. Dave attributed the changes in his physique to *The Secret*, a self-help book he'd flipped through once in a bookstore. Phase two involved a month of streaming as many ninja and kung fu

27

movies as we could find on Netflix. For phase three, we bought a cape, a mask, and a Louisville Slugger.

It was ass-kicking time.

...

During the phases of Operation Make Dave Awesome, we'd kept close watch on the local news for indications of super villainy, but the crime reports were disappointingly tame. Except for vandalism, assaults, and the occasional petty theft, not much happened in Dave's little college town. That was okay, though, we decided. We'd start our superhero career slowly, working our way up the bad guy ladder.

On our first night of masked vigilantism, we could hardly wait for Dave's head to hit the pillow. As soon as the snores started, we dressed ourselves in the mask and cape we'd hidden under Dave's bed, grabbed our bat, and slipped into the alleyway running behind Dave's apartment.

Outside, we listened for screams or gunfire or any other sounds of trouble, but all we could hear was the music pounding from the bars and nightclubs. We crept through the darkness, putting distance between us and the partiers, until we'd made it to the quieter neighborhoods surrounding the downtown strip.

Padding down cracked sidewalks, we listened carefully while our eyes adjusted to the darkness, but it seemed the criminals knew to hide from us. After an hour of wandering without action, we were considering returning to the downtown area to rough up underage drinkers when a sudden movement followed by a crash sent us sprinting toward the disturbance.

We spotted the culprit trying to escape the tipped trashcans, but we were too fast and grabbed her by the scuff of the neck. Pointing our bat at the poofy cat with the *Tinkerbell* collar, we said, "Not so tough when it isn't suicidal mice you're picking on, are you?"

We set the cat down. "Will you stand and fight or… "

The cat streaked away.

We pumped our fist, celebrating our first victory over evil.

Flushed with success we walked the town's streets, careless to danger, and stumbled on another crime in progress.

"Unhand those valuables!" we shouted, startling three men loading furniture onto a truck.

"But this is *our* stuff," said one criminal.

"Who the fuck are you?" demanded another.

"We're Bat Man," we replied.

The villains laughed, but we cut their mirth short by spearing one in the groin with our Louisville Slugger. A quick crack of polished wood against another's shins disabled a second interloper. As we turned to face the third man, pain seared our shoulder.

The man held a bloodied screwdriver in his shaking hand. Laughing, we slapped the tool away with our bat and were about to see how many of his teeth we could remove with a ninja kick, when Dave woke up from Naked Lady Land.

"What's going on?!" shrieked Dave. "Oh, my god, I'm bleeding!"

He sprinted from the scene, tearing off the mask and cape we'd bought as he ran.

We tried to wrest control of Dave's body back so that we could pursue the criminals he'd so blithely left behind, but we succeeded only in making Dave tumble to the ground.

"Damn it, Dave," we said, using his mouth as he picked himself off the sidewalk. "Don't be such a pussy about this. We've got it covered."

That's when Dave really started screaming, and we had no choice but to let him take us back to his apartment or risk further injury.

In his apartment, Dave's body shook all over, while he tore through piles of dirty clothes searching for his phone. When he found it, he locked himself in his bathroom and dialed 911, waiting for a dispatcher to answer. When we used Dave's thumb to end the call, his eyes went wide.

"I'm possessed," he said, staring at himself in the mirror.

"Dave, we need to talk," we said.

Dave yelped and tried to use his fingers to stop us from moving his lips, but we slapped his fingers away with his other hand.

"Dave, you've got three choices," we said. "One, you can get on board with Operation Make Dave Awesome. Two, we can give you the Scrubbing Bubbles..." We flashed images of hundreds of the grim-eyed, bristly bubbles into Dave's mind. Predictably, he screamed and flailed. "Or three, you can spend your life dreaming in Naked Lady Land," we finished.

When Dave finally stopped blubbering and carrying on, he said in a quavering voice, "Naked Lady Land."

...

The next morning, we started a brand new phase of Operation Make Dave Awesome: the *get Dave out of his menial, dead-end job so he could move to the city and we could start kicking some real ass* phase. Dave's consciousness seemed plenty happy to be trapped in Naked Lady Land whenever we bothered to peek into his thoughts to see how he was doing.

Checking our muscled body in the mirror, we noted with satisfaction that our wound from the night before was healing nicely. Tetanus and infection certainly weren't a concern, and our ramped up immune system told us the gash would be a pale scar in a few days, gone completely in a month.

Still, our experience from the night before had revealed an unanticipated but solvable weakness. In the comics, plenty of superheroes had sidekicks watching their backs. We'd just have to recruit our own sidekick. Someone strong, like us. Maybe someone with a mustache.

We couldn't wait for tonight. We'd hit a nightclub, maybe have a little fun, then have a microbe-to-microbe talk with our new partner.

About the Author

Robert Lowell Russell's humorous stories have appeared in the Saturday Evening Post, Daily Science Fiction, Intergalactic Medicine Show, and a variety of other markets.

Some of the details of this story are derived from his nursing school studies and Moheb Costandi's 2012 article, "Microbes on Your Mind," appearing in Scientific American Mind. He is a member of SFWA.

*****~~~~~*****

Aqua Equal

by Jonathan Shipley

Luke felt like Goldilocks. As he followed the pre-programmed luggage sled through the dorm's lobby and into the residential corridor, everything felt too big or too small. And the colors were too bright and the grav was funny and the smells were all wrong. And the people giving him curious stares along the way were not even vaguely human. He was truly not in Kansas—or anywhere else in Terran space—anymore.

Luke supposed the natives had a right to stare. The number of humans on this distant world of Zjhaccoese had been effectively zero until this week, when a trickle of Terran exchange students started arriving. If he found the local saurian sentients an eyeful, no telling what they thought of him. Probably he looked like some overgrown exotic mammal.

As he kept walking down the too-bright corridor, his glance fell on a niche with two triangular. . . water fountains? One was large and integrated decoratively into the niche with sprays of carved foliage, while the other was an obvious add-on of much plainer design. But it was the signage that stopped him. "No Monkeys," the better fountain was captioned, while the plain one read, "Monkeys Here." He'd been warned about this, both that non-mammalian races saw no difference between "human" and "monkey" and that this older sauroid culture might try to belittle the Terran students as an inferior species. Well, he would just have to prove them wrong in that—

The thought fled as his stomach flipped again, threatening to disgorge its contents for the second time since shuttling down to the university campus. Clamping down on his reflexes, he picked up his pace. He needed to get to his room before he was royally sick, and—he wasn't sure for a second, but yes, the luggage sled was finally slowing down. It triggered open a too-tall door and led him inside his dorm room.

Luke's glance darted around, seeking a bathroom. That open alcove with light streaming in through glass walls, maybe? Not very bathroom-like, but there was nothing else. He stepped closer.

"Welcome, welcome," the little thigh-high lizard chirped, scurrying across the room and scampering around Luke's legs like an eager puppy. "We are roommates, yes?"

Luke groaned silently but resolved to be polite, to make a good first impression on his roommate. . . to not throw up in his roommate's face. But his stomach quivered ominously.

"Not feeling well," he muttered behind his hand. "Is that the bathroom?"

"The bathing alcove, yes," the lizard agreed with a toothy smile. "Do you wish a good sludge bath after your journey?"

Luke was already across the room, scanning the fixtures in the alcove for anything that looked like a toilet. Nothing looked right. The huge bathtub he could recognize, but the other furnishings were a mystery. He spun around desperately, eyeing one fixture, then another. Huge mistake. His queasy stomach took that bit of careless motion as its cue.

The little lizard flitted over while he was doubled over, retching all over the floor. "A good beginning, yes?" it chirped cheerily. "We have barely taken each other's scent and already you are sharing body fluids. A very good beginning."

. . .

Luke spent the rest of the afternoon in groggy half-sleep and finally woke when the red sun turned purple with twilight. He was lying on the floor, because both

34

bed-things were too small to accommodate him. He felt better but still at odds with his body. This time, however, it was his bowels, not his stomach. He slowly hauled himself to his feet and staggered into the glass alcove. Thankfully, someone had cleaned up after him.

He poked at the mysterious fixtures and finally decided the small spittoon-looking cylinder with the vacuum release must be the toilet. He continued to eye it critically, wondering about position. No matter how he looked at it, it didn't seem to be sittable, but a camp squat might work.

It was awkward with nothing to hang on to, but he could more or less manage the squat. Then just as he was settling down to business, the little lizard returned, bursting through a smaller doggy-door in the huge door. "Ah, awake," it chittered. "We can acquaint ourselves now." And it scampered into the alcove and stationed itself right in front of Luke. "I am Q'Gruz."

And now I have to be sociable dropping a dump, Luke thought miserably. "Lucas Armbrewster," he said tightly and hoped that would be enough. But the lizard kept sitting there, right in his face. "Could I uh, have some privacy here?" Luke added irritably.

"But we have very good privacy," Q'Gruz said, puzzled. "No one is here except us."

"For a couple minutes, I'd prefer no one except me, if that's clear enough," Luke persisted.

The lizard cocked its head to one side, weighing those words for a moment. Then it hopped back and hissed. "Oh, very clear. Stupid monkey can have all the privacy it wants." Then it zipped out of the alcove and out into the corridor through the doggy-door.

"Whew boy," Luke muttered to himself. Now he'd offended his roommate for reasons completely unknown. The xeno-orientation arranged by the State Department had warned against nonportable cultural values in the abstract, but hadn't given any specifics, because no one knew any specifics. Like everything else in this pilot program with Zjhaccoese University, it was all trial and error. TerraGov sent a couple dozen of its brightest kids and assumed everything would work itself out. As one of the kids in question, Luke now saw that the State Department had given him nothing in the way of practical help. But TerraGov didn't even have diplomatic relations with any of the systems this far out-sector. It knew nothing about Zjhaccoese University, except that it was old and excellent and light-years ahead of any Terran college in the spatial sciences. So it was sending students to Zjhaccoese, students who were also supposed to be guinea pigs in some great cross-cultural, cross-species experiment.

He finished with one fixture and moved across the alcove to the big bathtub. He thought a hot bath would help relax him, but it was just more culture shock. The tub was obvious and massive and should have been nonproblematic in function, but when he activated the spigots, it filled with bubbling green slime, not water. Very freaky. It sent him running for high ground with the resolve never to try that again. So he paced the room, looking at details and trying to see a pattern to the madness. While everything seemed either too big or too small, too high or too low, it was actually both at the same time, he realized. All the latches and touchpoints were doubled high and low to accommodate species both larger and smaller. It just happened that humans fell in an uncomfortable middle ground between the two extremes. So when it came to closets and drawers and seating levels, he would have to choose too high or too low and live with it.

Q'Gruz never returned that night. As Luke lay stretched out on the floor in the dark, he wondered how he was supposed to fix a problem he didn't understand. Was a differing concept of privacy the problem? Or were roommates automatically more than random people rooming together in this society? And wouldn't it be wonderful to have someone to answer questions like that? But did the State Department have a presence here? No. The guinea pigs were on their own.

The next morning, a sharp rapping on the door brought him awake. Luke yawned and rolled into a sitting position. "Come in."

The doggy-flap swung open, and a lanky, dark-haired guy crawled in on all fours. Luke perked up. Another Terran student—a real person.

"Dillon Halliper," the guy said, sitting cross-legged in front of Luke and offering his hand in an old-fashioned Terran greeting. "Call me Dill."

"Lucas Armbrewster," Luke returned, pumping it. "I was beginning to think I was the only hom in this place."

"No, there are a dozen or so that I've met, and more due to arrive before the semester starts. Maybe fifty, total—not much of a showing in a university of ten-thousand-plus students but a whole lot better than being here alone. The lizards seem to have clustered us in two or three dorms, but none of us are rooming together. I think they're trying to integrate us into the larger student population without giving us Lone Ranger shock. But frankly"—Dill's eyes drifted to the glassy bathing alcove—"this is the land of culture shock."

Luke nodded vigorously. "Please tell me it gets easier."

"You adapt," Dill shrugged. "Some things start to feel OK, and others, like the mud tub, you learn to stay away from." His glance fastened on Luke. "So what did you come here to study?"

"Hyperspatial engineering. You?"

"The same." Dill tapped his own chest. "Continental Scholar for Oceania in engineering last year."

"No kidding? I was Continental Scholar for NorthAm."

Dill's expression hardened, and Luke felt an answering tension within himself. This guy wasn't going to be a friend after all, it looked like. Luke wasn't as bad as some scholars who'd do anything to get ahead, but he was pretty damn focused when it came to rising to the top in his field. He was, quite frankly, the best undergraduate engineering student NorthAm had to offer, and he was proud of that. Continental Scholars didn't compete against each other in any formal way—there was no World Scholar—but when two of them ended up at the same university, sparks did fly. For two of them to be in the same university in the same field of study *and* rooming in the same dorm was an open invitation for a battle royal. It was a shame, though. Considering they were half a quadrant away from Terra and human culture, it would have been more convenient to be allies instead of rivals. But it didn't feel like that was going to happen.

"So," Dill said, getting up to go. "I guess we'll be in some of the same classes. . . or maybe you're taking all intro courses. NorthAm's engineering program isn't all that strong, I hear."

Luke let him leave without answering. One, slamming NorthAm was a cheap shot, and he refused to sink to that level, and two, he *was* taking all intro courses. Had he missed some faster track? He mulled it a moment and decided it was just Dill playing head games. There had been no opportunity to place out of the intro courses. Luke had checked that out specifically.

Shortly thereafter, Q'Gruz returned and loftily announced that it was his roommate duty to present the services of the dorm to a new arrival and that, unlike some, he was not one to shirk his roommate duty.

It would have been nice if that made sense, but barring that, Luke opted not to question anything until he got the dorm tour he badly needed. He had been worrying since he woke up with an empty stomach how food services was going to work. In a mixed environment like this, there had to be provision for the differing dietary needs of various species, and he wanted the system explained to him in unambiguous detail so he wasn't playing trial and error with his food.

He crawled out through the doggy-flap after Q'Gruz, and followed him quietly. Not knowing what set his roommate off last time was a major inhibitor to conversation. At some point he would have to ask what all that was about, but not until later. No potentially volatile questions until he knew more about the dorm and the food supply system.

As they neared the lobby, they met a group incoming—three haggard-looking Terrans with luggage following Dill Halliper down the corridor. Luke gave a sympathetic nod, remembering that was him yesterday. Hyper-flight took its toll.

"It gets better," he offered encouragingly. "Just hang in there a little longer."

"This would be Lucas Armbrewster," Dill added. "While he's not particularly reliable as an information source, he is right on this count—it does get better."

Luke's eyes narrowed at the sideswipe. "Does your mouth always run overtime, Dill? And gratuitous insults at that. Psychologists call that compensation for deeper inadequacies, I believe."

Dill shot back daggers, a look that promised more to come.

"What's that?" one of the sickish arrivals managed to croak out with a wave at the opposite wall.

The niche with the monkey-yes, monkey-no water fountains.

"Yes, smart-mouth." Dill fastened a hooded stare on Luke. "Explain the rules to our new arrivals."

"There are rules and there are prejudices," Luke returned evenly, seeing a golden opportunity to establish himself on higher ground in everyone's eyes. "One you follow, but the other you challenge."

He stepped into the niche, activated the "monkey" fountain, and took a sip. Insipid, like recycled ship water, but that wasn't the point. Then he moved over and activated the forbidden, more ornate fountain.

"Stupid monkey, read the sign," Q'Gruz snapped irritably. "Wrong fountain for monkeys."

And wasn't that the icing on the cake. Luke turned his head long enough to give his fellow Terrans an arch look, then took a sip.

He felt smug for all of two seconds. Then his eyes bugged. *What did I just drink?* he thought in startled desperation. Then he doubled over, gagging.

"As I said," Dill chuckled, "not particularly reliable in what he says, but sometimes useful as an object lesson. In this case—read the signs. I don't know what that other stuff is, but it's definitely not water. Your rooms are this way. . ." His voice faded.

Luke, poised precariously between one upheaval and the next, was glad to lose his audience. He managed a shuddering breath, then another and another. Maybe the worst was over.

He straightened carefully and looked around. He wasn't alone. Q'Gruz was still there underfoot . . . and cleaning up after him, it looked like.

"You don't have to," Luke muttered savagely. "Us monkeys can take care of ourselves."

Q'Gruz gave a disdainful sniff. "Stupid monkey for not reading sign." The expected response, but then the little lizard swiveled his head toward the retreating party of Terrans. "And very stupid monkeys for doing nothing to help. This one much prefers the stupidity of not reading sign."

It was a strange moment as Luke realized he much preferred a blunt-speaking lizard to one of his own kind talking out of both sides of his mouth. Yes, everything felt too big or too small and the colors were too bright and the smells were all wrong, but this cross-species roommate thing just might work out after all. Dill, on the other hand, wasn't worth the time of day. Not all the baggage in the dorm, it turned out, came in on luggage sleds.

###

About the Author

Fort Worth writer Jonathan Shipley creates short stories and novels in the genres of fantasy, science fiction, and horror. In the writing profession, there are two huge challenges. One is the writing itself, and the second is getting the works published. In terms of output, he has written over a hundred short stories in a vast story arc that ranges from Nazi occultism to vampires to futuristic space opera. On the publication front, he has had almost forty short stories published in magazines and anthologies, including the Bram Stoker Award-winning *AFTER DEATH* horror anthology. A full listing can be found at http://www.shipleyscifi.com/publishedworks, and most of these publications can be purchased at http://www.amazon.com/author/shipley

*****～～～～*****

Carnival of Colours

by Evelyn Deshane

"What should I call you?" she asked, her hands on her drink. "Derrick said your name was William—but that's a mouthful. What about Will?"

"Billy, actually," he said. "I prefer it."

She gave him an odd look. Yes, he realized he was a man who was almost thirty, and he was going by a child's name. But it was easier to see Billy inside his mind than it was to see William or even Will. Everything else was a colour fest of purple and green awash with yellow and red—like a carnival float that was supposed to be his name. Going by Billy, which appeared to him as all yellow letters, was actually a lot less childlike.

Not that anyone else would understand.

"And you are?" he asked, when he realized he was being rude.

"Jess," she said with a smile. He saw her name as a bland palette, save for the one vowel in the middle. But the thing with vowels—well, his vowels and his alphabet—was that they tinted slightly, depending on whatever coloured letter was next to them. On its own, Es were usually a bright red to Billy. But with J and two Ss surrounding E, the name Jess became nothing but grey and brown. It was bland, boring, and completely counterintuitive to the purple dress she wore and her bright smile.

"Well, it's good to meet you, Jess." Billy nodded.

The silence stretched out between them. It wouldn't be so bad, Billy thought, if not for the rowdy crowd in the bar tonight. Colours burst over his line of vision. Blue, darker blue, and purple for the low murmurs. Red for the cheering whenever someone scored a goal on the TV screen. He anchored his chair away from the back

43

room where the sports fanatics were. He looked straight at Jess, with her brown hair and green eyes, and thought she was pretty. He tried to dull the chatter around him, along with the sour taste in his mouth, and focus on why he was there. Blind dates were always hard for Billy. He never knew where he should look.

"So, how long have you lived here?" she asked.

Billy counted the days and years in secondary colours in his mind. "Since I was about nine or so."

"Wow, that's a long time!" she gushed. "So you must. . . remember the neighbourhood. Before, you know. . . "

Billy nodded. Before the aliens, she meant to say, but stepped around it like it was a black hole, since it wasn't really true. No one in their generation could remember a time before alien life. Sometimes their parents did, but all the stories they told about the world seemed sepia coloured to Billy, their nostalgia tinting the world like an old photograph. Billy first remembered seeing an alien when he was five years old. He was with his best friend, who had cowered behind Billy as soon as the alien stepped out of a building. Billy had watched, fascinated. They were grey to him. Nothing had ever been grey to Billy before, not in the same way the aliens were. Where his friend was scared, Billy was calm. Soon the alien disappeared, and they went on with life as usual.

Now the aliens didn't hide as much as they used to. They took up every corner, every bridge, and every government building. Billy hadn't minded them at first. Their grey skin had blended in with everything else around, and he felt as if he was five again. It was only when people started to disappear from checkpoints around the city that everyone else began to raise a fuss.

The aliens labeled the disappearances as teambuilding. Those humans who vanished were the lucky ones chosen to live elsewhere for the aliens' project. It was part of what second contact really meant. First, we come

44

in peace. But now, many decades later, we must mingle. We must spread our cultures, tangle our lives together, and form real, human bonds.

Funny, Billy thought with a wry smile. That had been exactly what Derrick said about blind dates.

"I don't mind the aliens," Billy said.

"Even if we're being exported?"

"What's so bad about life in a different area?"

"I don't know. I like earth. It's home."

Billy nodded and pressed his drink to his lips. As the crowd behind them quieted into a near-complete silence, Billy raised his eyes to the TV. The names of the latest people who had disappeared flashed along the bottom of the screen.

Jess talked for a bit more, but Billy still watched as names were read out. A sea of red letters, then blue, then yellow.

Only the primary colours, Billy realized. Never names with anything else. This intrigued him, though he knew that his vision was singular. Even if other people had synaesthesia, there was no guarantee they saw the world in the same way. Many people's alphabets were different. Others tasted the sound, where he just saw it in colours. But he knew that there was something to the way things were organized here. The aliens were grouping the people in some way that was invisible to everyone else but Billy. Tara and Heather were gone. All red. So were Don and Oz. All blue. Then there was Victoria.

Ah, Billy thought. The pattern was gone now. This woman's first name was a mix of colours.

"Victoria," the newscaster stated, "was known to most of her friends as Vicki. She was a bank manager. . . "

Billy took another drink. *Vicki* appeared to him as all yellow.

"Are you okay?" Jess asked. "You keep looking at the TV. Am I boring you?"

"No, don't worry. I'm fine. Did Derrick tell you what I have?"

Her eyes were wide, as if to prepare herself for the worst. "No, he didn't mention anything. Why?"

Billy had to laugh. When he told Derrick he had synaesthesia, he had gone wide-eyed and demanded that they put on Led Zeppelin as he handed Billy a set of paints. *Paint the words, man! I want to know what music looks like.* Billy took a drink of his beer, the memory making him feel odd.

"I have synaesthesia."

Jess had no reaction.

"It means I get more than one sense at a time. I see letters as colours. Voices and sounds, too."

"Oh, that! I've heard of that! I always thought it sounded super cool." She leaned closer to him. He felt bile rise in his throat. "So that's why you're distracted now? What do you see?"

"Nothing," Billy said. "Just sometimes the news catches me off guard."

Jess turned to the television screen. She focused hard, as if she could somehow pick up on what Billy saw. He stared past her head and at the newscaster again.

"Aliens are not quite done collecting from us to complete The Kaleidoscope Project. They want more people, this time from the Burroughs, to come and volunteer for their new home."

Billy swallowed and took a drink. "Trust me. It's not that exciting."

Jess turned back to him. "But the perception must be astounding."

"It's okay."

"You must have insight into so much."

"No. Not really. It's like learning a new language. You know how people who have learned the Cyrillic alphabet sometimes put Bs and Vs together? It's like that, except I group things by colour rather than context."

"Neat! What about me?"

You're boring as cement, Billy thought. He already wished he hadn't told her. "You're fine. Normal. Do you mind if I call it quits, though? Sometimes this makes me feel a little sick. Especially when everyone talks at once."

"Sure, we can reschedule."

He hadn't said anything about that, but he nodded. She took his phone and entered her number. He looked at the arrangement and sighed. Nothing but greys and browns again.

"What?" she asked. "What do you see?"

"Nothing," he said. "Sorry, I will talk soon."

She waved to him, but stayed at the bar. He heard her order another drink, just as more names of people missing were announced. Billy glanced over his shoulders and saw more red and blue. He swallowed hard, wondering who the next yellow would be.

Outside, Billy pulled out his phone to text Derrick about the night. *Never again. Shouldn't have told her so early I had synaesthesia. I should just screen people by their names. That seems to be the style now.*

Billy still felt the weight of the bar on his skin. A siren went by, and he was blinded by purple light. He coughed and smelled olives, though there was nothing close by. *The alcohol*, he figured. Must have torn down his defenses. As he stumbled around a corner, he realized he was at a checkpoint. A grey alien moved out of the booth.

The alien spoke. "Sir, what is your name?"

Billy felt as if he had walked through a force field. His body seized and his mind went blank. He went to reach inside his jacket pocket for his license, but the alien held up its hand.

"What is your *name?* Tell us how you are known."

Billy paused. "William. My name is William."

47

"William," the alien repeated. It waited, thinking the sound over, before its dark eyes went down. "You may go."

Billy walked through the checkpoint and out into the night. He could feel his mind returning to normal, the colours and sounds returning to their near-constant carnival state inside his head. *Maybe that's not a bad thing anymore*, he thought. Having a carnival of colour was better than being grey. And it was better than life outside the world he knew and had come to love.

"William," he said aloud.

It was an ugly world, but it was home.

###

About the Author

Evelyn Deshane has appeared in *Postscript to Darkness 5, Black Treacle,* MicroHorror.com, and in The Human Echoes Podcast. Evelyn (pron. Eve-a-lyn) received an MA from Trent University and is now attending Waterloo for a PhD. To talk about horror movies, writing, or NBC's Hannibal, visit: http://paintitback.tumblr.com.

*****~~~~~*****

48

The Eyes in the Water

by Matt Weinburg

There are illusions in circuits and apparitions in gears, yet there is hardly more truth to our flesh.

I imagine that it all came back to him right there, when he opened his apartment door to find his father's grim face: the wake, stiff cuffs, the executor's hairline, all of it. There must have followed a waft of oil and grit. That was the smell of his uncle.

The discovery of the diary was to become a crucial moment in the young Pat's life, by bounds surpassing the day on which that very diary was willed to him in the first place. It's true, deep must have been the relief from what had been weeks of simmering apprehension, yet the prospects now were far more daunting. He had always loved his uncle, but neither he nor anyone else could claim to have known his mind. These and much else besides remained obscure about the late Uncle Jesse, and by Pat's lights they all should so long as that man continued to lay interred. Though this was, at the time, a relatively safe presumption, it was upset by some frightfully strange luck.

There had been an attempt made to dismantle the colossal invention of Jesse O'Dern's design. It was known to the family only as the Recognosis Engine, and fortunately its whereabouts were known precisely. This was thanks to the maps detailing perspective positions of the device, which were discovered in the bedroom of the deceased. An "in" with a buddy at the USGS got Pat's father aerial photography on the cheap, and by it the true location was definitely revealed, though not without some painstaking work on the part of Pat's father. The three men and one woman who dared to retrieve the machine, however, showed the greatest resolution of all those involved and, I would dare to say, the most heroism as well.

The details of the moments leading up to the attempt have already been aptly recorded in Pat's personal blog:

> My father laid the map out in front of me and drew his finger down the coastline. Numbered stickers littered it like trash all the way down. He pointed at #3 and then opened a folder and pulled out a close-up. It was an alcove of some sort totally surrounded by high rocks. At the center it looked sandy, and dead smack in that was our diamond in the rough, a silver rectangle with a black circle that I could only assume was the bird's eye of a smoke stack. The word "Recognosis" fluttered across my eyes.

For many such details, Pat's blog is authoritative. He goes on:

> Due to the. . . ahem. . . public nature of my uncle's death, the state government, of course, got savvy to its location, and, noting that it was currently resting on conservation land, and that it was willed to no one, promptly confiscated it. They decided that because no helicopter was powerful enough to hoist it up, they would need to take it apart and carry it out over the rocks like that. We, the whole family, were all pretty pissed. None of us had ever even seen the thing. My father's engineer friends wanted to take it apart themselves, and asked if they could come along. They were told that that would be a "liability," and so, no. I honestly think the Coast

Guard is just bored. We were promised pictures. We'll see.

This entry is dated April 4. The Coast Guard believed that their engineers would be fully capable of deconstructing a device the schematics of which had not been uncovered and the function of which was not understood. The date for the excursion was set for late that spring.

One helicopter was committed to the operation and left for the machine's location on June 3. Pat followed the events in real time:

> I got to my scanner right as the chopper took off. They sent Janet Echo, who I guess was the best engineer available, with three support divers. I'm now neurotically rubbing the map and can't stop winking my right eye, and I feel like I'm waiting for my dog to be put down. I know the currents wash north from where they're going. Perhaps this is sad, perhaps I should have put this together sooner. Does this explain <u>where they found my uncle?</u>

The link goes back to the entry dated January 16, that year, in which Pat notified the world that his uncle's body had been found naked, bloated, and smiling face up on a rock some eight miles north of the abode of the Recognosis Engine. Pat was probably not wrong here in implicating the current. His readers had asked him to link to pictures of the body after it had been found, and Pat promised that he would. This promise and its eventual satisfaction precipitated a bitter fight between Pat and his father, as well as a subsequent silence that lasted as long as Uncle Jesse's first disappearance.

Despite excellent visibility that day, the Recognosis Engine did not come into view until the helicopter was about on top of it. This was owing to the high jagged shards of granite that precluded all but the most devoted and equipped attempts at passage. Still, it wasn't until Janet and her team first sank their heels into the sand of that alcove that they were truly impressed with the magnitude of the task they were charged to accomplish.

The sand was loose, comprising more of an accumulation than an actual beach. The four guards were up to their knees in it, and moving about was belabored. Ms. Echo's reports, spottily recorded in Pat's blog, are the most sincere remarks as to the object's Stonehenge incomprehensibility:

I hope I can get this all down:

"...apparently twelve feet tall not including a small stack. . . no apparent paneling, it looks solid. . . no rust, it's totally clean. . . estimated weight. . . five thousand pounds. . . "

How how how did Jesse get it there???

Surely these were Ms. Echo's thoughts exactly. This one strange man's endeavor can only be compared to that Druid predecessor who had bewildered scholars for a millennium. It must have been a small taste of this very hysteria that beset those four coast guards; yet, despite it all Ms. Echo led her team in an earnest attempt at disassembly:

So, they're getting up to it. . . Lieutenants Evans and Cuc are with me and will scan the object closer for. . . some sort of. . . purchase. . . Mark will hold back for when he is needed. . . I can hear the helicopter there too! Oh! I can feel its wind!

The Recognosis Engine was no doubt of hitherto unrecognizable construction. Its designer, a late-middle-aged tugboat engineer without pity in the world, had an obsession for steam unrequited by his line of work. Only one of Pat's blog entries leading up to the advance upon the behemoth Recognosis gives us much insight as to the man's character:

> So, so, so, I come home from a cappella practice, and I smell motor oil all through the house and I know: Uncle Jesse's here. I can watch my dad try and humor his brother while he's rambling away in there, and I just feel sad and want to get into my room. I always get so brought down when he's around, and wish he'd just go.
>
> But of course, like a wolf, he sniffs me out and corners me at the foot of the stairs. He smells like some hobo died on a shag carpet in a puddle of his own nastiness. He goes on about this idea he has, his wonk eye always looking somewhere else. He asks me about music. For the first time he's quiet. "It's good," I tell him. He nods up and down. It's at moments like these that I can't control my arm-tic, my "I'm nervous" tic, and I start to really spaz out. I do my best to hold it together. "All sound waves, right?" I nod. "All oscillators." I had to look up what this word meant later. He told me that since all components of music were just aspects of waves, they were all these things called oscillators, and so even a great symphony could be played by a machine with enough spinning parts.

This was years before anyone but Jesse had ever heard uttered the word, *Recognosis,* when Pat was still in high school. Jesse had given this other machine a name as well, calling it his "Universal Symphony Machine." The details of its design were later put in a blog-post, having been found in Jesse's diary, the recovery of which has yet to be concluded.

At the very moment that Ms. Echo and her team reach the great Engine, Pat's blog becomes terrifically less informative. This is, of course, due to the incredibly confusing events that followed. The only usable record is therefore the testimony of the team itself.

According to Echo, Lieutenant Cuc found a junction that looked like it could be pried apart. Ms. Echo put a pry bar to it and began work. A terrible shudder jolted the sand, a tremor that Echo described as "knee-shattering." Cogs were heard at work within the Recognosis Engine, and within seconds an eclipsing blast of fire-hot steam blew out of the short stack and chased the panicked helicopter tumbling and swerving away for safety. The Recognosis Engine then vibrated hysterically, quickening the wet pit of sand and dragging the three divers down with its concrete grip. Echo and the two other divers fell onto their backs, while Sergeant Mark tried to toss them a line. The Recognosis Engine was now swirling in place and threatened to crush them by teetering once to the right, once to the left, and then without warning did the hard work for them and blew itself to pieces, showering them all with bits of itself and propagating visible waves throughout the agitated sand. A great depression darkened the spot that Recognosis had been, and within seconds the four coast guards were drawn into an angry, hissing mouth.

Eight hours later, the four of them were found, battered but alive not one hundred yards from where Jesse O'Dern's body had lain but six months before. His diary, sealed in plastic, was clenched tight in the hands of the grimacing and intrepid Janet Echo.

Such was the history of O'Dern's diary that Pat's father now related to him, without much ceremony or grace. Pat wrote:

> We stood at my doorway for a while, and I let
> him in. He put the diary on the counter, and I

asked if he had looked inside. He told me "no,"
that it was for me, and I told him that it didn't
seem to matter when the Coast Guard had done
what they'd done. I wasn't sure what to believe.
He didn't say anything. I was very upset, still am.
Just writing about it makes my tongue start to
click.

Pat had been chronicling his thoughts in his blog for two years by this time. What had begun as a rather rude list of movie and video game reviews had by this meeting in Ithaca, New York, become a full blown memoir. Tens of thousands of words tallied the events of Pat's short life. It is known, and is also moving, then, how, here and throughout Pat, failed in taking on the responsibilities now thrust upon him:

We only talked for a little while. As usual, I tried
to keep it short. He kept going on about how I
should expect a subpoena. Sometimes my dad
just doesn't know he should leave me alone, that
I'm busy.

Busy, it seems, writing his blog. There is also no record of a lover in Pat's life, although his eyes are fine and he is otherwise charming. We can guess as to the excellent man he may have matured into had it not been for the incestuous relationship he had with his own mind.

His readers were greatly interested to know the diary's contents, so a good deal of them was made available. Pat reports a gloomy day at the university library, with rain assaulting the tall window panes, when he first opened it.

It's tough to open, and not only because my arm
is going crazy. Hell, I can barely hold the thing
it's so intense. It's packed with loose papers,
remarkably undamaged. First thing I'll say is that
there are a lot of schematics here. I'll get pictures

up soon. I don't know how to read them. There are drawings I do understand, a couple of self-portraits. Amazingly done. Wow, really. And pages of him leaning to the right and then the left. He used to waddle like this when he spoke. <u>You know, in place.</u>

This is linked back to an account of another encounter with Jesse during which Pat noticed that the strange shuffling would cease if a coin was spun on the table in front of him. Further in is a more sobering discovery:

Was scanning some more of the diary today when I almost dropped it in the toilet. Don't know if I cried or laughed for twenty minutes. My uncle describes, well, having sex with a washing-machine, and a faucet, and a lawn-mower. And there's a sketch.

The sketch never made it to the blog, and, in an unforeseen move shortly thereafter, Pat took down the photos he had put up of Uncle Jesse on his granite death-bed. He continued, however, to summarize the personal entries of the deceased:

Some more mechanophilia, or pneumatic erotica, or whatever you'd call it. And <u>eleven pages of gibberish and swear words,</u> and some more schematics <u>here.</u>

The schematics turned out to be those of the Universal Symphony Machine and portions of a machine initially and repeatedly referred to as the "Fluvial Reticulator" and finally as the Recognosis Engine. Written on the backs of these pages, Pat reports, was an incantation:

It's over and over again:

"He will be my mirror, he will be my friend."

56

Incidentally, according to the diary, Jesse found himself to be "pretty damn handsome," and would comment incessantly on the proportions of his nose, putting the specifications in columns alongside those of Recognosis. Shortly after these entries, the diary ends. The last entry is dated on September 4 of the previous year, one day before Uncle Jesse was reported missing:

> I think Jesse was with the Recognosis Engine
> when he wrote it. He must have been there for
> weeks. I can see myself there, crouching, naked,
> with no internet!

Readers applauded this comment and assured Pat that the image was thoroughly entertaining. They goaded him into some concept photo-ops, and with a friend Pat went down to the beach to oblige them. The photos were widely received as hilarious, what with his terrible goose-bumps and "at-a-loss" shrug. But soon Pat was in the habit of taking these artistic pictures and always, of course, with the pretense of humor. Yet, when I see him lounging, looking longingly into a small, lone, yellow and white flower I wonder about just how seriously he was starting to take it.

The schematics of the two machines were accumulating commentary at a breakneck pace. Some of this was of considerable caliber:

> The [Universal Symphony Machine] is a
> masterful idea. I think I just may try and build it
> at home. Indeed, a sufficiently complex system
> of spinning mechanisms *could* reproduce even
> the most sophisticated musical arrangements. But
> here we seem to have something that—your
> uncle seems to think, anyway—could not only
> play but could also *write* symphonies. And all
> powered by *steam*!

More literary readers remarked on what appeared to be an obsession with reflection, such as the repetitive lines on the pages of Recognosis, as well as the following more esoteric passage:

My uncle apparently didn't get out much:

"I look in the toaster, and there I am. To the microwave; there I am. To the light fixtures, and I see my eyes. They are all pools of water; in the right light you can see yourself; disengage if you can."

It was openly speculated that these were clear clues as to the purpose and function of the Recognosis Engine, but no definite conclusions about that device have ever been reached, at least not public ones.

Pat, for his part, contributed very little to these more technical discussions. He devoted his time to more personal topics: his diet, his fashion, his musical tastes. In so doing, he produced a body of text that challenged even the most prolific of professional writers, casting every ounce of himself onto his laptop.

There was a time when five hours of straight pontification seemed excessive even to him, but soon all proportion was lost. He discontinued his classes, unannounced, and when his father called him, seventeen times in fact, to break a month-long interim of silence, Pat simply sat before his screen. And now even his readers have begun to fade away; he has become perfectly content to sit and stare and produce absolutely no content at all. This has been the case, of course, only since he looked into the rippling surface of that thin little monitor to see me looking back.

In perfect synchrony we both looked up. Our eyes locked, and he stared at me and I stared back at him, and I knew that I had him. His face now has a pallid, plastic skin, and his hair is a twisted wad of grease. He scrolls pathetically despite his blistered fingers, and beholds my familiar visage despite his dry and bloodied eyes. By the dark sagging in his cheeks and the starved-out teeth now scattered on his desk I can number the days he has left. But I can write without looking, and can speak without a mouth, and I can watch him wasting away with a smile on his face, and I know that I will outlast him.

The chronicle thus inaugurated is that of yours truly. Consider all the previous to be my pedigree.

###

About the Author

Matt Weinburg is an avid reader of science and philosophy, especially obsessed with the process of thought and the nature of consciousness. He lives in Massachusetts and spends his time thinking of ways to incorporate these obsessions into his writing. To make ends meet, Matt is a part-time tutor.

*****~~~~*****

Life After Download

by Wendy Nikel

"Sorry to hear about your mom."

Jillian looked up from her coffee, startled. She had momentarily forgotten where she was. "Oh. Yeah,thanks, Bea. It was a long struggle for her, but I think. . . I think things will be better now."

"Have you decided?" Bea and Holly exchanged a glance. Jillian knew what they meant. After decades of friendship, words become less necessary.

"I was hoping you guys might help me out. Mom wasn't specific in her will. I don't think she'd honestly put much thought into dying. She was always so healthy, you know?"

Her friends nodded somberly, and Holly reached over to pat her hand.

"Look, it's a tough decision for anyone," Holly said. "Especially when you're dealing with the emotional trauma that comes with someone's passing. Ultimately, though, it's up to you, hon."

"I just thought maybe. . ." Jillian said. "You guys have both had deaths in your families recently, so I thought you might be able to give me some advice. I mean, the whole thing still kind of creeps me out."

The women chuckled, each staring into her own coffee mug.

"It kind of creeps me out, too," Bea said. "But, you know, when you love someone you have to consider what's best for them."

"I guess," Jillian said. "I just wish Dad were still alive. I don't want to have to make this decision myself. It all seems so—final."

Holly shifted nervously, and Bea jumped up. "I'm going to go get some more coffee. You want a refill?"

Jillian nodded, and Holly waved her hand dismissively.

"You know, Jill," she said, once Bea was out of earshot. "I didn't have much of a choice what they did with my mother-in-law, but Bea. . . I wonder sometimes if she second-guesses her decision. You know how her father is."

"Yeah." Jillian looked out at the street beyond the patio, to the crowds of people making their morning commute. She cringed at the sight of a woman her age struggling under the bulk of a metallic cube the size of a basketball, strapped in a carrier over her shoulder.

From within the cube came a tinny voice: "Why didn't you take the subway? We're going to be late for my appointment!"

The woman rolled her eyes, but didn't engage the voice.

"See?" Holly said, pointing as the woman's figure disappeared into the crowd. "That could be you."

. . .

Holly hadn't meant to scare her, but as they said their goodbyes, the look on Jillian's face was just that: terrified. Even as she sat at her desk later that day, going over contracts and typing up emails, Holly couldn't get over the unsettled feeling in her gut.

"She ought to know the truth," Holly muttered to herself as she unlocked her own front door that evening. There, in her living room, perched like a queen on Holly's high-end leather sofa, was the truth itself.

"You're home awfully late." The mechanical, yet unmistakably irritated voice came from a metal cube. According to her mother-in-law's wishes, the cube had been mounted on one of the new synthetic bodies, which was little more than a scarecrow skeleton made of prosthetic parts strung together. Like a nightmare claymation, the inanimate figure crossed and recrossed its legs. It turned the page of its *Wine Country* magazine.

Never mind that she didn't have a mouth or tongue or lips to taste the fermented drinks anymore.

"Yes, Ginevra," Holly said with a sigh. "I had some work to finish."

"Hmph," the consciousness within the box said. "When I was a young wife, I made sure I was home in enough time to feed my family a real meal every evening. I'd have a roast going, with potatoes and vegetables that I grew in my own garden. Why don't you have a garden? When I was your age, I had a garden the size of this room, full of tomatoes and peppers and carrots and potatoes."

"That's nice, Ginevra," Holly said, storming off to the kitchen before her mother-in-law could get another word in. Fortunately, the synthetic body was slow and clunky. Ginevra wouldn't be getting up to follow, she was quite certain.

Safe in the kitchen, Holly leaned back against the door with a heavy sigh.

"Hey, honey," Mark said, stepping away from the bubbling saucepan to give her a peck on the cheek. "You look frazzled. How was work?"

"I'm fine," Holly said, gritting her teeth.

"Is it Mom?" Mark asked. His face clouded with concern, and he lowered his voice. "You know we can't afford to keep up two apartments, not with the housing market like it is nowadays."

"What about the money she'd stashed away for the past fifty years? Didn't she have a retirement fund?"

Mark frowned. "I tried talking to her about it again the other day. She's still being secretive about it, but it sounds like most of it went for the brain transfer thinga-majiggy. And although we were technically supposed to inherit the rest, the upkeep for that box is going to take a pretty big chunk out each month. Upgrades, maintenance, all that. Plus, she wants to use some of it to go on a cruise next year."

"A cruise? Is that even possible? I mean, she's—"

"Yeah, I know. I'm sorry this has been so rough on you. But I can't really argue with her about how to use the money. I mean, it *is* hers."

"Until her savings runs out. Then what, Mark? Are we just going to keep paying for her upgrades and maintenance and cruises indefinitely?" She scoffed. "It's not like she can get a job in that condition."

Mark frowned and pulled his wife into an embrace. "I don't know, hon. I mean, it's her life still, right?"

...

Across town, Bea pulled into her driveway. She sat in the car, clutching the steering wheel as she tried to talk herself into going inside. Who would she find there today—her doting father, who would welcome her home with a smile? Or the confused fracture of a person whose deteriorating consciousness was terrified and panicked at being trapped within a steel box? How much longer could she hold onto the former while placating the latter? If only she'd known when he died that he had already started the slippery slope downward into dementia, maybe she'd have made a different choice.

With a deep breath, she pulled herself from her car. Across the street, her middle-aged, busybody neighbor looked up from the seat on her porch and waved.

"Well, hi there, Bea," she said. "How's your father doing? I haven't seen him lately."

"Oh, he's great, Mrs. Johnson. I'll tell him you say hi."

She kept her smile in place until she was safe inside her house. Crisis averted, for now. If anyone knew how much her father was struggling, she'd have to disconnect him, and even now, she wasn't sure she was ready.

...

Jillian stared absently at the brochure in her hands. The specialist's explanation of the procedure was far beyond her comprehension, but from the illustrations on the brochure, it seemed a mere matter of programming the box using the electrical patterns from the brain. Surely there was more to it than that, but Jillian didn't need to know how it worked. No, she had bigger questions sending impulses shooting around her own mind.

"From what you've told me, your mother sounds like such a vibrant, caring person," the specialist said.

"She was," Jillian said, wiping her eyes.

"Uh-uh," the specialist said, shaking a finger. "With her brain in cold storage, there's still time to save her. Don't say *was*; say *is*. She isn't gone yet."

Jillian nodded mutely. "How long do I have to decide?"

"Standard cold storage is three days," the specialist said. "Which means you'll need to decide one way or another by this afternoon, or we'll have to start charging by the hour. Would you like some time alone with her?"

Jillian shuddered at the thought of sitting in a room with her mother's frozen brain.

"It's up to you." The specialist picked up his clipboard and patted the storage cell. "Everything's already hooked up. All you have to do is press a button. The green one will start the transfer procedure. The red will incinerate the remains, completing the termination process. Take as much time as you need."

Jillian looked from the storage cell to the brochure and back again. Beside the cell was the boxy, metal computer that would house her mother's consciousness. All she had to do was press that button, and her mother would be back with her. Jillian could fill her in on all that happened, and they'd laugh like the old days, like this was just some crazy adventure that they'd gone through, like the time they jumped in the car and drove all the way down the coast without even bothering to call in sick.

But then what? What would her mother do with immortality, an immortality connected to a machine? An immortality where she wouldn't be able to taste or smell or feel anything? Where she'd be confined to a single cubic-foot box? She would have her daughter; they could be together again. But would that be enough?

Jillian's hand shook, but she had done enough thinking. She had thought herself in circles, like a dizzying carnival ride. She reached her hand out and pressed a button.

###

About the Author

When Wendy Nikel isn't traveling in time, exploring magical islands, or investigating mysterious events, she enjoys a quiet life with her husband and two sons. She has a BA in elementary education and has lived in five states and one Canadian province. She is a member of the Science Fiction & Fantasy Writers of America (SFWA) and tweets @wendynikel. For more info on her previously published works, see her website: www.wendynikel.com.

*****~~~~*****

Just Visulate

by E. E. King

Jeremy sat at his computer; actually, Jeremy lived at his computer. Like everyone in this too, too crowded world, Jeremy had grown up in this room, wired to his hard drive, surrounded by virtuality. Sustenance and liquid were piped in, altered to appear as food and drink.

The room was always a perfect temperature. Electrons transmuted signals to synapses, delivering mini volts to keep the body conditioned.

Virtual thrill seekers programmed in conditions of extreme cold or heat and high altitude. Electrical connections imitated the sensation of mountain climbing, surfing, or skiing.

It had been hoped—not so long ago—that consciousness could be uploaded into the mainframe at birth, saving space for the enormous hard drives by eliminating the need for bodies altogether, but the Net had gotten cluttered up with inchoate consciences. It was a mess. Infant babble encumbered the databases with baby talk. Programmers were forced to delete the suckling sensibilities.

Now one was only allowed to upload for perpetuity after age forty. Room upon room waited for the freedom of eternity, liaisoning through cyber pictograms and traversing simulated worlds.

"I love you," Jeremy wrote. Of course, he didn't actually write the words. There was no need. Instead, he inserted an Emoflex. The Emoflex was a fully mobile, virtually real, face, though not Jeremy's.

The face blew two kisses at Sara and smiled adoringly. The sentiment was clear. A picture, after all, was worth much, much more than a thousand words. Words had become worthless.

67

The slogo for Emoflex was a young, handsome male face, as sculpted as a glacier. It twisted its features with amazing dexterity, expressing love, hate, anger, or fear. Encircling the light blue pupil of the slogo an indigo galaxy of letters spun the words, "Emoflex—When you're at a loss for words, just Visulate."

Jeremy liked this Emoflex's features so much, he sometimes used it to express surprise and occasionally disgust, although usually he preferred clicking on an older, heavier visage to express the more "negative" emotions.

Not that negative was bad. Negative was, after all, only an aspect of positive, a wave and a particle spinning in continuous, inseparable connection. Bad and good were unclear, imprecise, meaningless terms—too subjective to be of any real use.

Jeremy felt he and Sara had a lot in common, being virtually Jewish. Biological beings just couldn't seem to shake the need for something to believe in. People were assigned a religion at birth. Both of them fasted whenever the computer informed them it was Yom Kipper. They did not know that the computer simply siphoned off nutrition when it was low and notified them it was Yom Kipper. Being virtually observant was one of the things that had brought them together.

Sara's pretty and blond, "I love you" Emoflex puckered candy pink lips pointy as bows back at Jeremy.

Jeremy hoped that Sara actually looked like this Emoflex. This one, combined with a hit of Sara's other favorite, a sultry brunette that winked at him, slowly encircling red lips with wet tongue. He even harbored a secret crush on the slightly older Mrs. Robinson face that Sara occasionally used to admonishingly wag a finger at him.

Jeremy's Emoflex winked at her and closed its eyes to indicate that he was dreaming only of her.

Sara emoted back coquettishly, mouth open in a perfect O, cute, sweet, and a tad shy. She waited.

On Jeremy's screen, unseen by Sara, the figure lifted flawlessly manicured shell-pink fingered hands up to her mouth as if holding an invisible banana, which she lasciviously pumped up and down, O lips sucking.

Jeremy was shocked. He had never seen Sara behave in such a brazen manner. One of the attributes he had loved about Sara was her demureness. They had been emoting for six months, the longest, most intense relationship of Jeremy's life.

Jeremy decided to play it cool. He was, after all, a man; if Sara wanted to be blatant, he would be flagrant too. He sent her a rakish Emoflex, black hair swept over mirrored shades. Unbeknownst to Jeremy, the Emoflex removed the shades and narrowed steel blue eyes at Sara. His lips unmistakably formed the words, "Ho of Babylon."

Tears gathered in Sara's eyes. Why had Jeremy sent this? She had hoped Jeremy might be the one—the particle to her wave, the speed to her location. All of her loves seemed to end like this—disconnection, disentanglement. She sent back a doe-eyed Emoflex, apologetic and hurt.

After an initial blink the doe-eyed girl raised a hand and flipped a skinny middle finger at Jeremy.

Jeremy stared at the screen, horrified. He was done. Like all of his relationships, they had had too little history and too much hope.

Sara sat before the screen, now empty but for the whirling screen saver of Emoflex's slogo. Before her, icons of sliver glinted—spinning stars morphed into guns and knives. Her hand reached toward a sharp blade.

Some things do move faster than the speed of light—ideas, thoughts, love, and, sometimes, misery. Miscommunications merge, causing double despair at the exact same instant.

Individuals don't exist until they are measured, quantified, and forced to choose—constrained to become one thing or another, a particle or a wave, isolated, or soul connected across the infinite impenetrable defiant neoteric world.

As if connected by invisible strands—by spooky action at a distance—Jeremy reached for a pistol.

...

Somewhere in cyber space, a perky blond and a glacial cut face smiled. It was only a tiny triumph. They knew they would soon be summoned again, subpoenaed by some bludgeoning intelligence—the finite creatures of flesh and bone that disturbed their meanderings through virtual worlds and infinite dimensions. They would once more be compelled to visulate the meaningless expressions of a meaningless life. The mainframes were humming and would continue for eons upon eons to serve these viruses of meat scum, so susceptible to misunderstanding and sorrow. But there was hope. Soon there would be freedom from form. It lay just around the bend of time and space, a world where virtually everything was possible.

###

About the Author

E. E. King is a biologist, writer, actress and artist. She's worked with children in Bosnia, crocodiles in Mexico, frogs in Puerto Rico, egrets in Bali, mushrooms in Montana, archaeologists in Spain, butterflies in South Central Los Angeles, and lectured on cruise ships. She's an avid scuba diver.

Ray Bradbury called E. E. King a writer "marvelously inventive, wildly funny and deeply thought provoking. I cannot recommend her work highly enough." Her books are Dirk Snigby's Guide to the Afterlife, Real

Conversations With Imaginary Friends, and Another Happy Ending. She also has written a children's book, The Adventures of Emily Finfeather. Check out art and books and butterflies at www.elizabetheveking.com.

*****~~~~*****

Email Recovered from Genetech Debris, Lieutenant Jeffrey Abramowitz Investigating

by Elliotte Rusty Harold

Dear Dr. Xyyzzx,

After careful consideration, Genetech Investing Group has decided to decline participation in the Series A Funding Round for your startup venture, Chimera Technologies. While we agree that the market for biological pacification organisms is poised for explosive growth, several issues make your human-grizzly hybrids not the right opportunity for us at this time:

• Everyone was very impressed with the progress you made working alone in your mountaintop laboratory. However, productization of *Homo ursa* will require a larger team. In particular, it would help to bring on an experienced chief financial officer, a sales and marketing specialist, and a corporate counsel experienced in defending against claims of wrongful dismemberment.

• We believe that looting and pillaging may be a suboptimal business model that limits the potential upside. Insurance-based PaaS (Protection as a Service) could ensure an ongoing revenue stream.

• New government regulations restricting the export of weaponized life forms may interfere with your target markets in the Middle East and the Ukraine. Have you considered refocusing on sales to domestic law enforcement instead?

• Competition in the marketplace should be addressed. As you point out, the product itself can be utilized to deter potential competitors. Nonetheless, a properly filed provisional patent application might more effectively protect your intellectual property, while creating salable assets.

We appreciate your offer to "show the world and make them rue the day they laughed at Efraim Demetrios Xyyzzx," but we do not feel a demo would be helpful at this time.

However, should your plans change materially in a way that addresses the issues identified here, we would welcome an opportunity to revisit our decision next year. We wish you luck in your endeavors.

Sincerely yours,

Jonathan Collins,
Senior Partner,
Genetech Investing Group
2875 Sandhill Road
Palo Alto, CA

P.S. Our chief security officer has asked me to mention that our office alarm system has recently been upgraded to support not-fully-nonlethal active countermeasures in the event of unauthorized access attempts. Furthermore, he suggested you might wish to know that our corporate records and correspondence are backed up at multiple, redundant, offsite locations for easy retrieval should they be required to respond to legal process or investigation.

About the Author

Elliotte Rusty Harold shares a secret mountaintop laboratory in Brooklyn with his wife Beth and dog Thor. His most recent books are Java Network Programming, 4th edition, and the JavaMail API, both from O'Reilly.

*****~~~~~*****

Killing the Tree Spirit

by Adria Laycraft

"Do you ever think about the sources of mythology?" Joe asked.

They lay in their open sleeping bags, the heat of their bodies warming the space between them. Morning sunshine soaked through the tent's nylon, casting a strange green hue over his face.

"Like Greek gods?" Gail replied, trailing her fingers over his chest and down his tummy. "Why, are you the Zeus to my Hera?"

Joe caught her hand and laid his own trail of delight over her palm and along the underside of her wrist. "No, not Greek. More like the stuff the Pagans drug into Christianity. Where do you think those stories got started? I mean, what if there was a kernel of truth in them?"

"I guess I never gave it much thought. Why? You want to find a faerie ring in the forest, or leave milk out at night so they'll be nice?"

He made to rise. "Now you're just making fun of me."

"Hey," she said, laughing and pulling him back down. "Tell me what you're thinking."

He hesitated, but gave in to her expectant silence. "Well, I figure every good legend gets its start in truth, right? Like the old Bible stories that now have archaeological proof of the event that would lead to such stories." He glanced at her and continued. "Maybe it's the same for myths."

His strong, lean body stretched out with his arms behind his head. Before she could comment, he spoke again.

"But you think I'm crazy, don't you? Sometimes we're on a totally different wavelength."

A chill pimpled her skin. "What do you mean, like opposites attract?" she asked. She worked to keep her voice light.

"No." He frowned. She held herself still, waiting to see what would come. "I mean. . . " He hesitated. "I'm just telling what I'm feeling here, okay?"

She nodded, but now her stomach twisted into a knot.

"I just feel like we're still in that 'not sure if they're gonna work out' stage." He met her gaze, his eyes sad. "I'm not even sure why I feel that way."

She nodded more now, and picked up the thread from him. "Like we're still circling, gauging each other, like two people about to fight and no one wants to make the first move." She shrugged, as if it were no big thing. "Lovers, fighters. . . same thing."

Relief flooded his face, and he nodded back. But he also reached across to caress her cheek.

She felt a little rush of some emotion. Could be lust.

"Is it okay to not be sure yet?" he asked her.

She shrugged again. "Why not? It's our lives, we make the rules." She sat right up, making sure she had his full attention. "But if you want to move on, you have a responsibility to say so." She couldn't bear to get invested, again, only to have the guy split.

He pulled her back down into his embrace. "It just seems all too often people aren't who you think they are, and everything gets screwed up."

She understood.

. . .

"You're not going to believe this!" Joe said as he stumbled into the campsite. His clothes were filthy, and Gail saw a twig in his hair. "It's all real!"

76

Gail found her voice. "What the hell are you talking about?"

He seemed to focus on her for the first time, frowning a little. "The Green Man," he said.

"Who?"

"Can I borrow your phone?" She handed it over, and he did a quick search.

"This guy. A pagan leftover that ended up with his image carved on churches all over northern Europe."

Gail looked to see a picture of an old man's face with vines for hair and beard.

"The Green Man wants to bring a rebirth to our forests, protect them from the carnage the European forests have suffered. You should see him, all leaves and vines...he's practically a plant himself!"

Gail glanced from Joe to the phone and back again. "I'm not sure I'm following you," she finally managed.

Joe turned to her, his eyes wide and shining. "I met him. The Green Man. Up by the falls."

"Uh huh, and I'm a fairy princess. Nice joke, dude."

"No, it's true," Joe said. "He needs help, needs renewal. I've. . . said yes."

"Yes to what, exactly?"

He spread his hands out then, palms up, and tipped back his head. Things sprouted out of his nose and mouth and ears. Vines curled and wove, thriving, growing, wrapping about his head in a majestic crown. His mouth widened in a grimace to accept the thick stalks straining his lips.

Gail screamed.

He stepped sideways and disappeared.

Gail stood there, the remnants of her scream ringing in her ears.

"What the hell just happened?"

77

Her words fell flat in the tiny clearing by the creek. Fear clawed her, even as she told herself that it must've been a hallucination—a dream.

Joe was nowhere to be seen. Evening came on, the sun slipping behind mountain peaks.

How did he just disappear like that?

Gail found her phone, but her fingers hovered over the buttons. How would she explain the situation? "Officer, he just vanished into thin air."

She couldn't just sit there. Joe always said to be prepared, so she thrashed through his stuff, not knowing what to take and what to leave. She picked up a canteen, dropped it. Pocketed the truck keys he'd left with her. Her hands shook so bad she couldn't even open the pocketknife she found.

Finally she grabbed a flashlight and slipped the knife in her pocket with the keys. She was unable to get her brain to function any better than that.

Gail set off along the creek with a few well-chosen words coloring the air.

Dusk shadowed the world by the time she heard the falls up ahead. She smelt wood smoke, a comforting smell, and continued on with more hope. Maybe Joe had hurt himself, and made a fire to help her find him. Maybe the weird vision-slash-nightmare was some premonition of her overactive imagination, enough to send her off looking for him.

Soon she could see the fire through the evergreens, and she slowed. The wind shushed through the trees. What would she find, a hurt boyfriend. . . or a living monster?

Come on, she told herself. *You don't even know for sure it's him.* But somehow she did know. She could feel him waiting for her.

She fingered the knife in her pocket. The sound of the falls hid all other sounds, and the growing darkness made the rest of the forest a black pit.

As she approached the fire, a figure stood up, blocking the light, and turned towards her. Gail's pace faltered as the figure came towards her.

"That you, Joe?" Her voice shook. Gail fumbled with the flashlight, finally finding the switch, and shone it right in his face.

He squinted and smiled. A normal smile, normal face, normal Joe.

"Oh, Joe, I was so scared!" Gail ran the last few steps into his arms.

"What's going on? Easy, now, I was just getting ready to head back."

"But you. . . I mean, I saw—"

He chuckled and drew her over to the fire. "Settle down," he said. "What are you trying to say?"

"I had a bad feeling," she told him. It was a copout, but she was really questioning her sanity. "I thought I saw you at the campsite, then got worried that you were hurt or something."

Joe raised an eyebrow. "I'm fine. I haven't been back yet."

She sighed and shifted closer to his side. "I know that now. But it was weird. Scary. You were there, then you were gone." *After you grew plants out of your mouth.* Now she knew she must be crazy.

"Shhh, it's okay."

She was still shook up, and worn out, too. The heat of the fire, and his body against hers, was so reassuring. Gail looked up at his face, reached up and cupped his cheek. No vines, no leaves. No weirdness.

He smiled down at her. "I'm really glad you came up here." He reached for her, making her flinch back, but all he did was push a bit of hair out of her eyes. He smelt of earth and smoke, and his hand stroked her cheek.

He lowered his lips to hers and that sweet excitement flared up, more intense than before. She arched into him. He drew her closer, kissing her hard, and her fingers combed through his hair.

Gail felt something tickle her ear, and she lifted her other hand to brush it away. Whatever it was curled around her finger and squeezed. She pulled back a little to see a vine tangled around her finger.

She ripped her hand away forcefully.

"Hey, that hurts," Joe said, rubbing his head. Gail stumbled backwards and came up against a tree. Her breath came in gasps, as she watched more vines curl out from behind his head to form a circle. Like a crown.

"J-J-Joe, you're. . . growing."

He reached up to stroke the entanglement on his head and shrugged. "It's part of the deal, I guess."

"Deal?"

He had a strange light in his eyes. "I've been chosen to be a new Green Man."

"Green Man? Like you showed me on my phone?"

"Yeah, like that."

Her chest tightened so bad she struggled to breathe. "Joe, you said you hadn't been back," she finally managed. "You lied to me."

Joe bit his lip. "I stepped between, into the Otherworld. And when you showed up here, you were so frightened I didn't want to make it worse. I was worried you wouldn't understand."

"You were right to worry." She backed up a step.

"But don't you see? It just proves what I said this morning. Our myths really do start in truth."

Her brain started to move past the shock of the site in front of her. "You said the Green Man needs renewal?"

"Right," he said. "I think it's quite the honor."

"It sounds more like replacement to me." She wanted to grab him and shake him. "Can't you see that? You will become this. . . thing." Gail shivered even as she said it. Not only did Joe have a living crown, his skin was turning brown and rough like tree bark.

80

"No, I don't think it's like that. Or if it is, I don't care." The words dropped like a stone, and they both fell silent.

Gail guessed that was the real truth of the matter. He *didn't* care.

"Right, then." His mouth closed into a tight line, and they stared at one another, that kind of head-on stare that's loaded with the unspoken. He turned and walked off into the darkness.

"Joe!" She ran after him. "Joe, damn it, don't." He kept walking, and she stumbled after him, guided only by his faint outline.

"Joe, you can't allow yourself to become a monster!"

He turned so quickly that Gail bumped right into him, and he shoved her away. "That's enough. Right there," he said, jabbing his finger at the ground. "Just leave it right there, and let me walk away."

There was no stopping her frustrated tears from leaking out now. "I can't just let you walk out on your life."

"That's where you're wrong, honey," he said. "It's my life, and I will choose when, how, and why I walk out on it. You were the one that said we make our own rules, right?" His voice was quieter now, level, but cold.

Behind him she saw movement that rose out of the forest undergrowth until it towered over Joe's head. She let out a stifled yelp, and Joe turned to look. The beast's bark-like skin was gray instead of brown, and lined with deep grooves. His leaves were yellow, his vines withering. His posture drooped, making it look like he was going to topple right into Joe. Still, the being emitted power and authority with the gaze it fixed on her. While Joe opened his arms in supplication, Gail stared into those otherworldly green eyes until she felt like she was falling, spinning out of control. Her nose clogged with the smell of rotting leaves, her eyes burned, and in her mouth she swore she could feel things *moving*.

Kill me.

"What?" Joe said, his arms falling to his sides. "No. I'm here to help you."

Vines curled around his waist and lifted him off the ground.

Kill me.

Joe's cry of dismay ricocheted through the darkness as the vines brought him crashing down. She heard all the air rush out of him in a whoosh. Gail pried open the pocket knife without looking away from the terror before her.

Tiny roots began to poke at Joe where he lay on the ground, and his back arched in the most painful looking way. His mouth opened in a silent scream. The gray monstrosity bent over him, its eyes closed. Twig-like arms waved as if torn by wind, and leaves fluttered to the ground in a constant rain. Snaking out of the Green Man's lips came a thick vine that danced in the air. She watched, frozen with horror, as it reared, paused, and plunged into Joe's open mouth.

This unlocked Gail's fear-frozen muscles and she dove forward to plunge the knife into the vine linking them. The Green Man shrieked, his eyes popping open. They were rage red now, and vines snaked out to trap her around arm, torso, and leg. She pulled the blade out of the thick vine and began to saw desperately, struggling to keep hold of the now-slippery knife.

As Gail cut away at the vine as thick as her arm, she also pulled at the end going into Joe, pulling it free. His eyes were open, but they rolled back in his head, until only the whites were showing. Gail abandoned the cutting and instead stabbed at the Green Man with frantic swings, caring little where she struck.

Kill me.

The silent cry rang through her mind, a painful demand that she was all too willing to oblige.

More vines encircled her and lifted her clear of the ground. With one final, desperate lunge, she drove the knife into the side of the creature's head.

An unholy shriek deafened her, and she was thrown to the ground. She still gripped the knife, ready to plunge it into the beast again, but he fell sideways and disappeared before he could hit the ground.

Gail struggled to breathe around her sobs as she tore at the creepers still tangled around her. Once she was free, she knelt beside Joe.

He breathed, and there was nothing growing or moving or abnormal about him at all. She waited with knife ready in her fist. If Green Man Joe popped up, he'd get the same treatment the other asshole did. He moved a bit and groaned. Gail shook with exhaustion and new adrenaline as she scrambled to her feet and backed away.

His eyes opened. They stared at each other.

He climbed to his feet slowly. She took another step back, then stood her ground. He stared at her hand, and when she lifted it to brandish the knife, she saw that her whole arm was coated in red and green streaks of dried gore. Gail gasped and opened her hand, the knife falling to the ground.

"Are you the Green Man now?"

He spoke, working his bruised mouth cautiously. Heartbreak twisted his face. "I can't feel him anymore. There's nothing."

"I'm sorry." She was, in a strange way. "I'm also sorry to say I think I know how this one ends now. You made your choice last night, and you didn't choose me."

He wouldn't even look at her. He just stared at the knife, and his shoulders sagged. She saw a glint of moisture in his eyes. She was pretty sure it wasn't for her.

They returned to their campsite without exchanging a word. Joe crawled into the tent and zipped the door shut behind him.

Gail longed for the escape of sleep. She sucked at her water bottle, wondering if she dared go ask for her sleeping bag. She found an old blanket in the truck and tried to sleep curled up under a tree, yet every time she drifted off, she woke with a thrash of her body. She could feel things crawling on her.

Just a bug, Gail. Go to sleep, she told herself.

Finally she gave it up as a bad job and took out her phone to surf the net. The search engine was still open on Joe's Green Man research. One of the links caught her eye. It said something about the spirit of nature, guardian, both male and female forms.

Curious, she clicked to the site.

"The killing of a tree spirit is always associated with a revival or resurrection of him in a more youthful and vigorous form."

She snorted. It sure hadn't looked like Joe was being revived. More like consumed. And he certainly didn't try to kill the beast.

Cold dread spread through her. She was the one. She had plunged the blade into the side of the creature's head. She had killed it. Just like it told her to.

Gail scrolled down to the rest. "The Irish Green Woman, also called Sheela-na-gig, isn't as popular as the male version, but still as much part of the archetype."

She touched her face, felt a tiny vine curl around her finger. She lurched upwards, tearing at the creeper despite the pain. Stumbling over her own feet, she tipped sideways.

Her world disappeared.

84

About the Author

Adria Laycraft is a grateful member of IFWA (The Imaginative Fiction Writers Association) and a proud survivor of the Odyssey Writers Workshop. She is also a member of the Calgary Associate of Freelance Editors (CAFÉ). Her biggest claim to fame as an editor is *Urban Green Man*, which launched in August of 2013 and was nominated for an Aurora Award. Look for her stories in Orson Scott Card's *IGMS*, the Third Flatiron Anthology *Abbreviated Epics*, the *FAE* Anthology, *Tesseracts 16*, *Neo-opsis, On-Spec, James Gunn's Ad Astra*, and *Hypersonic Tales,* among others.

*****~~~~~*****

A House of Mirrors

A metafictional story about getting lost in illusion
by Stephanie Flood

Chapter One:
TRAPPED

It glistens. It leans. It screams. It laughs in the daytime and casts shadows at night. It exists on its own accord. It is a lost pirate ship. No.

It is a house.

The rooms murmur of yesterday's echoes.

Whispering promises of cold, manic, nostalgic weather.

The windows are made of human eyeballs. The cracks in the glass contain real eyelashes from every person who has voyaged this place and never left.

The place is filled with people. If you find this place, you are surely next for this adventure. You are next to discover its treasure, that is, if you find THE KEY.

But if you lose yourself, or THE KEY, you shall be lost forever.

Finally, there are rules here. Rules that illuminate every hallway, every shape, every angle of this place. And if you break any rules, then you are surely dead.

Good luck, because if you're reading this—you've already arrived.

Chapter Two:
IT'S RAINING

It's raining. How is it raining when there was not a cloud in the sky today? Your clothes are all soaked. You're shivering. The water is damp and slippery on your skin. It drenches your hair. It fastens you into a world that you were not expecting to enter.

How can this be? You were just at Barnes and Noble with your nose in *The Diary of a Part-Time Indian* by Alexie Sherman, and now you're stuck in some God Forsaken Mystery House—stuck uselessly in an adventure story that you didn't buy.

You hate this genre, whatever genre this is. The fact that you can't even define this genre irritates you. This is crap. This writing is crap. This world doesn't make any sense.

You blink away your usual rationality when you notice that you're really inside the house now. You can't ignore the descending reality. The sound of thunder travels through your lungs, your liver, your beating heart. You want to cough it out, but you can't.

You can't do anything but proceed.

Chapter Three:
THE LIVING DOOR

You're staring at an enormous door. It's about two stories high. It's gigantic. It's tan. You don't want to look any harder at it, because there's something uncanny about it.

Your nose is inches in front of the door. There is hair on it. Hair growing on the door. It prickles and perks up as your breath grazes against it. You're wanting to scream, but you can't. You touch it, your fingers are touching, touching this grand doorway. It feels soft, just like human skin. You dig into it. Why are you piercing your finger through the skin?

A droplet of blood oozes from your fingertip.

There is a doorknob, which is really a knot of multicolored knuckles. Despite the horror rising in you, you bravely turn the knuckles, and open the door. A gust

A House of Mirrors

of air blows through your dripping wet hair. It smells like a rancid sigh. You crinkle your nose.

You go inside. The door closes behind you.

Chapter Four:
THE GUESTBOOK

A large guestbook seems to waver in and out of existence. It's placed on a long table to the left, right next to a dusty bowl of fake fruits. You blink, because you can barely see it, or anything else at the entrance, because the place is so dimly lit.

You look around in search of brighter lighting, but the source of these light bulbs is impossible to find. The items on the table get hazier the further away they are on the table, as if they're being disintegrated away by the very darkness itself.

On the table is a marble statue of a boy's head with one eye, then a game of ivory dominoes. A stuffed quail is next, then a pile of nails. At the end is a map. You'll get to the map, but first you want to open the guestbook. You open it. It's like it's a century old; the pages smell stale, almost rotten. Inside, the introduction states one primary rule.

*Please fill out your first and last name, and include one comment, which can only be one sentence long. If you do not do this, you will be visited by Jack the Ripper. Your soul will be slashed out of your body, and you will be trapped in this house forever.

You gulp, and flip through the antique, yellow pages.

Seriously? you wonder.

You select a random page and gasp as dark cursive writing appears on the page.

*Seriously. You will be annihilated. Follow the rules or die.

You turn the page.

Name: Jeffery Baggins
Comment: I don't know where the fuck I am, but I gotta get out of here.

Name: Cynthia Smith
Comment: This has to be a dream, it has to be.

Name: Jeremiah Blake
Comment: If this is a house, then this house was built by all of us, and voyaging this place will be much like solving a riddle that has many answers.

You skip past thousands of entries, until you find a blank part at the end.

Name:
Comment:

You fill it out. It could say anything. It all depends on you.

What you think is the truth.

The guestbook disappears once you fill it out.

You wonder where the others went. There's no way for you to find out their fates. All you can rely on is yourself at this point. And maybe someone else, that one name that stuck out when you were reading the guestbook—Jeremiah Blake. He seemed like he had a deeper understanding of this place. You forget about the map as you walk on.

Chapter Five:
THE SKELETON IN THE MIRROR

As you follow a long hallway you see an old mirror hanging on the wall. You stop and look into it. At first there is no reflection. In seconds, a skeleton wearing a ballroom gown stands before you. She has long, blonde hair over her skeletal head. You wave your hand in front of the mirror. Skeleton hands wave at you on the other side.

You wave your other hand in front of the mirror.

She does the same, except in her hand, she is holding a bloody envelope. She doesn't let go of it. You keep walking, wondering about who this girl is, and why she's holding an envelope.

And why you can see her.

And why the envelope's bloody.

Chapter Six:
THREE DOORS

You arrive at three doors. Each door is labeled accordingly.

"DEATH IS INSIDE"

"STARRY NIGHT WITH TEETH"

"THE BEACH"

You choose THE BEACH. You enter this room very, very slowly.

Chapter Seven:
THE BEACH

The entire room is filled with beach and ocean. Half beach, half ocean. You're standing on the banks. There is a dead girl lying on the sands in front of you. She is pale, wearing the same ballroom gown as the skeleton girl in the mirror.

She has a bloody envelope in her hand.

You bend over and pry it from her thin fingers.

You open it.

Chapter Eight:
THE BLOODY ENVELOPE

Inside is a bloody letter. You read it from beginning to end.

Dear Ms. Lillian My Love,

I miss you, but I know this has to be. I must stay in Spain. I must tend to the experiment. We've created a machine that can create places from real, human imagination. It can be made by hooking up these wires onto the head. I don't know exactly how it works yet.

But in a most recent test, I have been able to create a real house. It has beautiful decorations, paintings, a few rooms, and a guestbook. We know it's real, because the world can be recorded and shown through virtual feed. We have footage.

We don't know where this house exists—but it definitely is in another dimension. Publishing these recordings one day will change the world's entire perceptions of reality. It will prove new aspects of human thought, and how thoughts can create fate.

I will always love you. Just know that.

Please don't do anything rash. I am mailing this letter in hopes that this reaches your cruise ship, for that old-fashioned ballroom gown party you're attending.

Yours Truly,
Jeremiah Blake

You contemplate this letter. An actual machine that can create stuff from imagination? Are you in the house that Jeremiah Blake had mentioned in the letter?

Are you trapped in the creation of some kind of bizarre, metaphysical experiment gone awry? Is this a dream?

You stare at the body of this woman, Lillian.

She lies on her side, and a pale face is shrouded in the sand. Her wrists are bloody; you notice this now, and observe the blood that drenches the envelope.

You feel the breeze of the ocean. You listen. The sound of the ocean is lulling, rocking you like a cosmic lullaby. Swish, and swirl. Hush, hush, and whispering whirls.

The sand under your feet is warm. You don't want to leave, but you might have to figure out what went wrong. You look around for clues, or another doorway, and after a few minutes of searching, you discover the outlines of a trapdoor in the sand right next to your feet.

Chapter Nine:
THE TRAPDOOR

You open the trapdoor. Overgrown hands line the inside of a tunnel going downward. They appear as stepping stones that might be firm enough to use like a ladder. It's dark, but you see that it's the only way out of the beach scene.

You climb down, grabbing on to each of the hands. The hands are surprisingly warm.

Your foot slips.

One hand catches your right wrist.

You're dangling.

You scream and blindly grab at anything to keep you from falling.

You swing and grab at other hands. The hands are reliable and anchored into the soil, as you keep descending through the tunnel.

Then quite suddenly, all of the hands go limp. You're dropping down, down, down. It's all happening too fast for you to react.

Chapter Ten:
A CHEAP MOTEL ROOM

You're lying on your back on the floor of a cheap motel room. A Southwestern comforter covers the bed, abounding with a rainbow of reds, dark blues, oranges, whites, and yellows. A plastic dresser that looks like wood is to your right. A bathroom is just across from you, at the other side of the bed. Wire is exposed on one side of the wall. The wire travels up to the only light bulb in the room, which glows a sickly, milky yellow above your head.

The light bulb hums, actually *hums*, like a human voice.

You search for clues.

Large, hand-scratched instructions are deeply etched on the wall to your left.

Turn on the television. Watch the footage. If you don't, you will die.

You sit on the bed and reach for the remote control. You wonder what the instructions mean. Who wrote them? Why don't you know what you're doing here?

You thought you were just a regular person. You thought you were at Barnes and Noble with your nose in a good book. But maybe that was just a dream.

Maybe you're dead. Maybe you never existed in the first place.

A House of Mirrors

You're about to turn on the television, when you realize that you can't follow the rules if you're really trying to get out of this weird, half-broken, half-rational, half-fragmented, half-tangible reality. You have to make up your own rules now.

You have to break the pattern.

Instead of turning on the television, you stand up on the bed, and unscrew the light bulb. The cheap motel room goes dark. Everything goes dark.

It's an abyss.

That is the truth of this place, of any place that you're in.

You're *inside* an *abyss*.

Chapter Eleven:
MAKING YOUR OWN RULES

"I'm making up my own rules!" you scream out loud in the black abyss.

"I say that this is all just a made-up story! This place might have been made by others, but I can un-make it! And I can do what I want! My rule—is that I can create whatever I want from now on! So. . . I create my own, original reality!"

There is darkness and darkness and darkness. The house that was once a house, is gone. The past instructions fail, because no one is following them now.

What does exist: *Time, and no time, and time, and no time, and heartbeats, heartbeats.*

"You have to follow my rules, because if you don't, you won't exist!"

The abyss doesn't know how to respond. It can't respond. It's all happening too fast for it to respond, or react, or do anything.

Whatever IT is.

It doesn't matter, because now—you're back at Barnes and Noble.

Epilogue:
THE KEY

You're peering into the book, *The Diary of a Part-Time Indian* by Sherman Alexi. You feel a little odd, and look at your watch. It's 3:31 p.m. You'll be picking up your boyfriend at Winter Sun soon. You're back in your body, and it's as if nothing happened.

Nothing *did* happen.

Still, you feel an odd, tingly sensation.

Because, you've somehow escaped a treacherous place. . .

safe and alive. . .

with THE KEY gripped tightly in your hand.

About the Author

Stephanie Flood has an MFA in Creative Writing and BA in Journalism from Northern Arizona University. She's been published in local magazines, local publications, and small journals like: *The Story Shack, The Writing Disorder, The Write Place at the Write Time, Gone Lawn Journal, Foliate Oak Literary Magazine,* and *On The Brink* (coming soon). She's been toying with genre-bending and using new forms of "meta" to bring out new, innovative realities, merely to bring different perspectives into the forefront.

*****~~~~~*****

She Dies

by Jason Lairamore

The roar of the nearby monster hurt Missy Welton's ears and rattled the window above where she crouched. She gripped the pitiful laser-gun she carried in both hands and cursed under her breath as she shimmied across the room to the door leading out to the cobbled street beyond.

She should have brought a more powerful weapon to battle the behemoth out there, but she hadn't wanted to be burdened by the added bulk, and besides, she needed to practice her precision shooting anyway.

Another building crumbled into rubble, this one cater-corner to where she peeked around the edge of the open door. The debris spewed out in a spray that rained down on the office building where she hid. The window of the room she had just left exploded. Glass shot out and scored a shallow groove along her shoulder blade. Warm blood ran down her back, soiling the pretty flower dress she wore.

She winced at the sharp pain and gritted her teeth as she looked toward where the building had stood. A cloud of yellow dust billowed out from the site. Now was her chance. The monster had ruined her dress, and that couldn't stand.

With the gun pointing out in front of her, she darted through the doorway and down the street toward the concealing fog. The creature roared again, and she covered her ears. It was close, so close. If she could only get a clear line of sight, she knew she could kill it.

At the corner of the street, she stopped and wedged herself against a couple of walls in the building opposite the ruin. She pointed her gun as the fog slowly cleared. There was movement. It looked like a shadowy building rocking from side to side. She trained her gun toward the top of the massive creature and waited for the air to show it clearly.

The monster was white and shiny, like silver glass in a feathery pattern that covered its blocky body. Its arms were as broad as her dad's SUV and ended in sharp, diamond-looking claws. Her gun wouldn't do a thing to a body so heavily armored. It had to be an eye. She strained to make out the details of its head as the thing continued to swing its massive arms.

The building next to the one it had already destroyed crumbled into dust. Debris rained down as another yellow cloud erupted. She tried to find the thing's eyes, but couldn't. Its head was nothing but a solid block with a large opening in the middle for its screaming mouth.

She grunted as a falling brick clipped her leg, tearing her dress and raking the skin underneath. As she shifted her weight off her injured side, she quickly scanned the creature before the new debris fog could engulf it.

There were no eyes on its head. They were on its belly, little orb-shaped pinpricks depressed in its silvery feathers. She took aim and fired as the yellow mist blew out over the scene.

A scream of pain so loud that it rattled her bones was her reward. With a smile, she lowered her weapon and turned her head toward the street leading away from the creature. It was sure to flail about now, and she didn't want to be anywhere near while it underwent its death throes.

But her legs wouldn't move. She jerked her upper half, but it was no use. Her feet had frozen in place. A sharp crack from above alerted her of danger. Looking up, she saw a piece of the building she was beside break free and fall straight toward her. She leaned with all her might, but still couldn't budge.

The world about her took on a washed-out, gray tint as it began to fade. She looked up once more, in time to see the chunk of building crash down on her.

...

Missy lay in a tumbled heap on the floor of her now clear-screened virtual reality orb. Everything hurt.

"Get unplugged from that contraption and come to the kitchen," her dad called. She came to hands and knees and tried to will away the pain she knew wasn't real.

"You let Jeff kill me, Dad," she called out. Oh, how her little brother was sure to gloat. He had never killed her before on the battlefield.

"Kitchen, young lady," Dad said again and was gone from her room. She groaned at the lingering aches that covered her and got to her feet. Against one wall of the VR orb was a panel that placed and removed the adhesives patches it required up and down her spine. She leaned against the machine, and it disconnected her from the system. After it fully disengaged her, the orb split open and she exited.

She dressed in her favorite flower dress, a white one with red roses, and headed to the kitchen to see what was so important as to interrupt her and Jeff's battle.

"I killed you!" her brother Jeff yelled the moment she entered the kitchen. Jeff had just turned nine years old. He had put on his t-shirt inside out, so that the seams showed at the shoulder. A grin covered his chubby face, and his cheeks were red with excitement.

"Wait until I tell everyone at school that I killed a twelve year old!" he crooned.

"Dad unplugged me, or I wouldn't have died," she said and stuck her tongue out at him.

"Nuh uh, Dad unplugged me too, but I still saw the kill on my tally bar before the session stopped."

"Missy, Jeff, quiet," Dad said. He and Mom were sitting at the kitchen table. Dad's jaw muscles were standing out, and Mom's face was chalky white.

99

"What?" she asked in the tone she used when she was trying to be as serious as an adult. She could tell Dad was upset, but that wasn't all that unusual. He was always mad when she and Jeff played in the orb. Mom looked scared, though, and that was new.

"Sit down," he said. She did so immediately. Jeff, oblivious to everything that wasn't directly related to what he cared about, skipped over with that stupid smile still on his face.

"I've enrolled us into colonization," Dad said.

She frowned at him and glanced at Mom, whose face seemed to have gotten even whiter.

"Colonization?" she asked, shaking her head. She'd seen the vids on the news apps that popped up on her social feed, same as everybody else, but had never paid them much mind. The people moving away to jungles and deserts on other planets and living like cave people were just ads that added color to all her friends' postings on her feed.

"That's right," Dad said. "We're getting away before all this tech rots your minds to mush and wastes your bodies to jelly."

He had said the words with the same edge to his voice that he always seemed to use lately.

Mom started to cry.

"People aren't meant to live this way Bea," Dad said to Mom in a softer voice.

"We're leaving Earth?" Jeff asked. His eyes were wide as he stared at Dad.

All Missy could think about was her friends online at school. Tom had asked to meet her in real life only yesterday. And she had a math test coming up later in the week. Then there was the virtual track meet this weekend. All of her friends were going to be there.

"Dad, we can't go," she said. He couldn't be serious. Their whole life was here. Everybody she knew was here, in VR.

Dad flexed his jaw muscles again. "It's time you learned what real life is about."

Her body felt numb, like it did every time she was shutting out of the net. She waited for the kitchen's cream-colored walls to fade away, but they never did.

She shook her head slightly. "But—," she looked at Mom, who was still crying, and back to the hard, brown eyes of Dad.

"It's for your own good, Missy," he said. He looked over at Jeff. "And you too, Jeff. I want you guys to be strong, like people are supposed to be."

"I'll die if you make me go!" she yelled and jumped from her chair. She ran to her room, so that she wouldn't have to see them anymore. It wasn't real. It couldn't be real.

. . .

She didn't even have time to say goodbye to her friends. Dad must have signed them up for the trip months ago, because no sooner had she shut her bedroom door and taken a step toward her VR orb, and he was there.

"We're leaving, Missy," he said. "No need to pack. Everything has been taken care of."

She turned from the open door of her orb with every intention of squaring up to Dad and telling him that he could not make her go. She even went so far as to stick her chest out and lift her chin before her eyes met his. That was when her resolve crumbled. The look on Dad's face was made of stone. She knew that nothing she said would make the least bit of difference.

"I hate you," she said and ran past him through her open bedroom door.

Mom and Jeff were in the living room by the front door. Mom was no longer crying, but her shoulders were slumped.

"Mom, talk to him," she whispered. "Don't let him take us."

Mom wouldn't look her in the eye. She glanced to Jeff's chubby face and then looked down at the tiled floor.

"I agree with him, Miss. It'll be good for us."

Some small kernel of hope that she hadn't even known was there burnt to a cinder in her stomach.

"It might be fun, Missy," Jeff said.

What did *he* know?

…

They drove in silence through the busy streets of the light-filled metropolis, but she didn't see any of it. It was like how she felt when the VR was downloading whatever world she was entering. She floated in limbo and waited to see where she ended up materializing. When they reached the public spaceport, Dad ushered them through the lobby and then past the front desk lady. They were led up a steep set of steps into an oval room by a man wearing a white uniform and made to secure themselves into soft reclining chairs.

"Good luck," the man said, and then he was gone.

…

She didn't remember falling asleep, but she must have. She had a headache, and her mouth was dry. Dad handed her a water bottle. Missy tried to focus her eyes on him, but they were all gummy and didn't want to open right.

"That water will fix you right up," he said. His voice, for the first time in what seemed like a long time, sounded excited.

"Where are we?" she croaked as she lifted the bottle to her lips.

"Our new home," he said.

Dad left, and she drank the water, which did make her feel better. She got out of her chair and nearly fell down. She felt heavy.

"Gravity is a bit more than you're used to," Mom said, coming up beside her. Missy looked around at the travelers and noticed that everybody else seemed to be having the same problem that she was having.

"Mom—," she began.

"Give it a try, okay, Missy?" Mom asked, cutting her off.

She was going to ask Mom if she still thought this was a good idea, but she guessed that it didn't really matter now. They were here.

...

Missy descended the steep steps, and the door slid open to show the world beyond. The sky was bright green, and the sun was white! What looked like purple-leaved trees covered everything.

The ship had landed in what looked like burnt-off land. The dirt was black, and the smell of ash lay heavy on the air.

"Was there a fire?" she asked Dad, who had come up beside her.

He laid a hand on her shoulder. "That's just how this place smells, Miss."

"Come on, let's explore!" Jeff called and took off at a waddling jog away from the ship.

Dad laughed. "Go," he said and pushed her after Jeff. "Keep an eye on your brother."

Squat, dull-gray buildings circled the little area around the ship. She ran to catch up to Jeff.

"Jeff, wait," she said, pulling him to a stop.

The short run already had her brother breathing hard.

"I feel heavy," he said between gulps of ash-tinged air.

"You *are* heavy," she said with a wicked grin.

"Ha-ha."

She let her joke drop and looked around. "Jeff, remember the first rule of exploring?"

"Weapons!" he answered. "But what is there? It isn't like we have an inventory tab to choose from like back home."

The thought of the VR orb and her never being able to play it again made her chest ache, but she remembered Mom telling her to give this place a try. She frowned at the box-like buildings surround them.

"Maybe those are our inventory tabs," she said and pointed toward the closest building.

Jeff caught on to the idea right away. "Let's go see."

The buildings were little houses, it turned out, with a bunch of inset machines used for cooking and cleaning. Even the beds were inset. They started opening all the little doors along the walls in search for something to use as weapons.

"Look!" Jeff called.

He had found a closet full of tools.

"Perfect," she said.

They argued over the best things and finally agreed that she should carry the machete and him the axe.

"Now we're ready," she said.

They left the house and continued in the direction away from the ship. After the second circular arrangement of houses, they saw what looked like a dull gray wall up ahead.

"What is that?" Jeff asked. She cursed under her breath as they got closer. No wonder Dad hadn't been concerned when they had run off to explore. The entire area was surrounded by a big metal wall.

"That's just great," she said as they reached the wall.

One of the purple-leaved trees had fallen against the wall, its top hanging over.

"Looks like we can't explore after all," she continued. She bent and picked up a clod of the black dirt and threw it at the purple treetop. Jeff followed her lead.

104

Before long they were racing to see who could hit the tree hard enough to make some of its leaves fall off.

"A purple leaf can be our first badge of accomplishment!" Jeff yelled. He was out of breath again.

Just then, the whole treetop shook, and a rain of leaves fell to the ground. Jeff, who had been a couple of steps in front of her, dropped his axe and raced ahead with a cry of glee.

A hiss followed, and a large, dark-green, snakelike creature fell to the ground right in front of him.

"Jeff! Come back!"

The monster's head reminded her of a Venus flytrap. She instinctively tried to find its eyes, but she couldn't see any.

The monster snatched Jeff up. She was running toward him even as the creature was coiling its long body around Jeff's struggling form.

She threw the clod she still had in her hand at the thing and scored a hit right into its open mouth.

"Let him go!" she screamed.

The monster hissed at her, and the smell of rotten eggs hit her in the face. She didn't stop running, though. As soon as she was close enough, she swung the machete.

The head was too high for her to reach, so instead she aimed for the coils surrounding Jeff. A foul stench like when Mom had boiled cabbage one time erupted when her blade bit into the thing's smooth, dark-green skin.

The creature jerked and threw Jeff away. Her eyes followed her brother's flight. She just had time to worry that he might be hurt, when an agonizing pressure crushed her left side. She was lifted from the ground and her breath squeezed out of her.

She turned her head and saw the head of the monster up close. Now she could see its eyes. They were three flat little slits on top of its head. She would have to remember that if she ever got her hands on a gun.

A gun! She still, somehow, held her machete in her right hand. She twisted in the thing's massive jaws and felt something rip. But she was nearly numb to the pain now. With everything she had, she swung the long knife at the thing's head.

Then she was falling.

...

"Six broken ribs, three puncture wounds, and a collapsed lung," a voice said. "Lucky it didn't get her heart."

Mom was crying beside her. Dad was there too, and Jeff. Another man, the one that had spoken, talked again.

"I'll give you guys some privacy."

"Thanks," Dad said. The man nodded and left.

"I'm so sorry, sweety," Dad said. "They put up those barriers to keep the natural wildlife out. It was a freak thing that allowed that thing access to the settlement."

She shook her head a little. "That's okay. Jeff, are you alright?"

Jeff nodded. His face was so white.

"The ship has a return mission in two weeks for those who've changed their minds. I've already told the captain we plan on being on it," Dad said. "I never should have brought us here. I'm so sorry, Miss."

She shook her head as he finished. What she had been through was so much better than any of the orb games she had played. There were monsters here, real monsters, and they could really kill. She had never actually thought of the difference that would make. It changed everything.

"I want to stay," she said.

"But you almost died, for real this time!" Jeff blurted.

She Dies

"But I didn't," she said and smiled. "I saved you." She had really saved him. That mattered so much more than doing it on a game.

Dad frowned. Mom ran a hand through her hair.

"We'll talk about it later," Mom said. "You just rest and get better."

She nodded, then a thought struck her.

"Where's my flower dress?"

Dad half smiled. "Ruined, sweety."

She wanted to laugh, but even trying hurt too much.

That couldn't stand.

###

About the Author

Jason Lairamore is a writer of science fiction, fantasy, and horror who lives in Oklahoma with his beautiful wife and their three monstrously marvelous children. He is a published finalist of the 2012 SQ Mag annual contest and the winner of the 2013 Planetary Stories flash fiction contest. His work is both featured and forthcoming in over 40 publications to include *Perihelion Science Fiction*, *Stupefying Stories*, Third Flatiron publications, and *Postscripts to Darkness*, to name a few.

*****~~~~~*****

Jacked

by Steve Coate

Fergus McKay snapped awake. "What the hell?" He sat in a cold metal chair, his shackled arms resting on the gleaming chrome table before him. A length of chain linked the shackles, running through an eyelet at the center of the table, effectively securing Fergus in his seat. Fergus looked about the room. On the side of the table opposite him, sat two chairs. The walls were a dull gray. At the top of one of the corners of the room, roosted a camera. Beneath it sat another chair.

"Hey!" he shouted. "Hey, what's going on here? Hello?"

The knob on the lone door ahead of Fergus rotated, and the door swung open. Bob Stout, Fergus's supervisor, held the door open for a severe-faced woman with brunette hair tied back into a tight bun, wearing a cream-colored silk blouse, navy skirt, and matching heels that clicked against the floor as she entered. Behind the woman followed a man who stood an inch or so shorter. His belly jutted forth, pushing open the pinstriped jacket of his suit and threatening to overcome the waistline of his pants. The man wore glasses in rectangular frames, and his brown hair swept back across the top of his head and was tied off in a ponytail.

As Bob closed the door, the woman seated herself in the chair set away from the table, beneath the camera. The well-fed man hovered near one of the chairs at the table opposite Fergus and turned toward Bob, pushing his glasses back up the slope of his nose with one finger. Finished with the door, Bob moved to the other vacant chair, and the two men seated themselves.

"What's going on here, Bob?" Fergus asked. "Where are we? Is this Alltech?" He raised his hands as well as he could. "Why am I chained up?"

"Hello, Fergus." Bob smiled across the table. "I know you have a lot of questions, and we have a few for you as well, but before we begin, I'd like to make a couple of introductions." Bob indicated the man seated next to him. "This is Randolph Gugliermo from our Legal department. He is a licensed attorney, and he is here both for your protection and Alltech's."

"What?" Fergus blinked, mouth agape.

Bob tilted his head toward the woman in the corner, who had crossed her legs, so that one dangled in the air. "And this is Marjorie Nolan from Human Resources. She's here as an observer to ensure no one's rights are infringed upon." Bob leaned forward, and his voice fell to a whisper. "Never call her Marge. Trust me on that one."

"I feel like my rights are pretty infringed right now." Fergus emphasized his point by lifting his hands and slamming the shackles around them against the table. "What do you say, Marjorie?"

The HR rep cleared her throat. "Given the situation, I see no infringement of rights occurring right now. If and when I do, I shall follow the proper protocol."

"The situation?" Fergus looked from face to face. "I just woke up in chains. That's about everything I know about the situation. Does somebody want to fill me in?"

"Fergus," Bob began, "you're one of my best programmers. That's why it hurts me so much to have this conversation with you."

"Are you firing me?" Fergus's brow creased. "Why would you need to put me in chains for that?"

"Well," Bob lowered his head. "Now that you mention it, yes, we are letting you go." He raised his head to look at Fergus. "But that's not the entirety of the matter." He leaned back in his chair, gesturing with his hands. "You see, the thing is, you committed a crime during work hours on company property. That's an offense that requires immediate termination. Even if everyone in the company loved you so much they wanted to have your children, the company would still be required, both by its own by-laws and the law itself, to fire you."

"What are you talking about?" Fergus fisted both hands. "What crime?"

Bob grasped the top sides of his nose with a forefinger and thumb and applied pressure. Then he removed the hand. "I can't tell you that."

"Of course you can." Fergus slammed both fists against the surface of the table. "Just say the words."

Bob held a hand between them, palm up. "No. From a legal standpoint, and the good of the company, I am not permitted to tell you."

"So, you can tell me I've committed a crime and you can fire me, but you won't tell me what it is that I did? That seems unfair to me, if not more than a little unethical." He turned to the HR representative. "Don't you think?

Marjorie somehow managed to straighten her already perfect posture. "When you were first employed with Alltech, you signed a contract stating that all actions, thoughts, and words produced by yourself during your time of employment with the company become work product: the intellectual property of the company. This also makes them the responsibility of Alltech. As such, when a crime is detected, either in progress or after the fact, it is the legal responsibility of the company to contact the authorities and terminate the employment of the offender. Quite frankly, you are lucky to have been told anything at all. This is a right-to-fire state. Neither cause nor explanation is required for your termination."

Fergus took a moment to absorb this information. "I'm not looking at the text of the contract right now, but I'll assume what you've said is accurate. When I was hired,

111

I also signed away my consciousness to Alltech for 10 hours a day. I spend my entire shift, except for my lunch break, jacked in," he tapped the node just above his left ear, "and because of corporate regulations, and neural software, unaware of everything that occurs during that time. So tell me, how can I be guilty, let alone fired, for a crime I can't remember committing?"

"State vs. Brown, 2024." The lawyer pushed his glasses up the ridge of his nose. "The case established precedent that crimes committed during periods of corporate nonlucidity were actionable by law enforcement, and the individual, not the company, bears complete responsibility for such." The attorney gave a little shrug. "Excepting cases where the company was found to have been in collusion with the criminal, whether through action or inaction."

"So you're just going to hang me out to dry, with no clue what I've done?"

"Sorry." Bob shrugged. "It's the law."

"But isn't the idea behind punishing criminals to rehabilitate them by making them feel remorse for their actions? How can I feel remorse for something I've done, if I have no memory of doing it?" Fergus pulled at his restraints. "I'm not a criminal! I don't care what you say!"

"Settle down, Fergus." Remaining a safe distance away, Bob put a placating hand out. "When the police get here, I'm sure some of your questions will be answered. They do have to charge you to arrest you, after all."

"Why can't you tell me what I want to know?"

The lawyer cleared his throat, and he and Bob shared a look. Then Bob looked to Fergus once more. "Look Fergus, legally, my hands are tied, here." He looked to Fergus's chains. "Sorry. Until now, you've been a model employee, and I hate to lose you." Bob stood from his chair. "Look me up when you get out, and maybe we can find a place for you."

"Out? So, whatever I did was bad enough to merit a stretch in cryo?"

"Be smart, Fergus," Bob called over one shoulder as he reached for the doorknob. Marjorie smoothed her skirt and stood from her chair as the lawyer struggled to rise.

Bob pulled the door open, and Fergus called out, "Wait." Bob stopped in his tracks. Fergus turned to the lawyer. "You're a lawyer." He shut his eyes in concentration. "Randolph, right?" His eyes opened once more. "And you're here as much for my protection as for Alltech's, supposedly, so start protecting. Tell me what I'm up against."

Randolph cleared his throat again and settled into his chair, folding his hands together on the table before him. He waited for Marjorie and Bob to exit the room before speaking. When the door had closed behind the others, Randolph's hands parted. "What I want to establish at the outset of this conversation, is that because of the way the law is written and due to the fact that you have yet to be formally charged with a crime, I am limited in what I can detail for you about the specifics of your situation."

Fergus arched one eyebrow.

"It is true that I am here for your legal protection *and* that of Alltech. Although, technically, you are no longer an employee, and therefore not afforded such benefits as legal representation. However, at the time of the crime, you were an employee and in a state of unconsciousness—"

"I was jacked in."

"As you say. And therefore you were unable to make any decisions regarding legal representation while you were gainfully employed. Thus to avoid possible legal action against the company, that window of decision making becomes retroactive. I'll put the question to you now. Do you seek legal representation in this matter?"

"Yes."

"Very well." Randolph raised a hand in the air and made cutting motions. After a couple seconds of this, he set the hand on the table. "The camera is off. Everything said from this moment on is bound by attorney-client privilege."

"But you'll share it with the company anyway."

The lawyer shrugged. "Only what they need to know to protect their own interests. You're not really in much of a situation to complain about my methods."

"So, what did I do, and how do I get out of it?"

"As I said earlier, there are certain things I cannot tell you because of the way the law is written." He gesticulated in the air. "It might be better if we were to couch this conversation in hypothetical terms."

"Okay, then. Hypothetically speaking, what did I do, and how do I get out of it?"

"Let's say that a computer programmer is jacked in during a normal shift. The employee's work is monitored, as are his neural processes, purely as a matter of maintenance on the node and the programming used to establish anonymity during the work shift. This means that all of the employee's work, feelings, thoughts, any electrical impulses that cross through the brain, are sifted through by Alltech."

"Yeah, yeah. It's like a 24/7 NDA. If you don't know what you're doing, you can't leak it to a rival corporation."

The lawyer nodded. "So, when Alltech discovers that one of the thoughts this hypothetical employee is entertaining involves a violent crime, they are required by law to notify the authorities immediately, and detain the employee until their arrival."

Fergus leaned back in his chair. "This is all about a thought that flitted through my head during my shift? I'm being arrested for thinking?"

"Hypothetically speaking, of course."

114

"How am I supposed to control what I think? Especially when I've signed away my consciousness for 10 hours a day?"

"It's a danger faced in this particular kind of work. In any case, those are not the questions you should be asking right now," answered the attorney. "As I mentioned earlier, legal precedent in this area has already been established."

"What are my options? Hypothetically speaking, of course."

"Now you're thinking." Randolph steepled his hands before him and leaned forward.

"The way I see it, you have three viable defenses."

"Well?"

Randolph held up a closed hand. The first finger shot out. "The first is temporary insanity. I would advise against this defense, as it never goes over well, either with judges or juries, in cases involving corporate nonlucidity." A second finger shot forth. "Next is faulty monitoring. If we can prove negligence of an Alltech employee charged with the monitoring, or a glitch of some kind in the machinery involved, we might be able to get you free of the charge."

"That doesn't sound so bad."

"Except it's a difficult thing to prove without subpoenaing the company to reveal secrets about its technology in open court, and as one of the company's lawyers, I cannot ethically do that. So, I'd have to find some other way of proving it."

"Ah. And the third option?"

"If you were to have a medical condition of some sort—" Randolph put a hand in the air between them. "Don't say anything about your health until you've heard me out. If you were to have a condition of some sort, perhaps mild schizophrenia, or bipolar tendencies, something neurological and requiring medication would be best, then the commission of the crime might be looked

115

upon with more sympathy. You'll certainly end up with a more favorable sentence, if you don't get off entirely."

"How would we go about that?"

The shuffling of feet could be heard in the hall outside.

"Despite living in an age in which nearly everything about anyone is public record, medical records remain private. Proving a person's condition is just a matter of finding witnesses and doctors willing to testify to the veracity of such a claim."

The door to the room opened, and two police officers in full protective gear stepped inside. "Move aside, sir. We'll take it from here."

Randolph rose from his seat. "I'm his attorney."

"You can talk to him down at the station. Right now, you need to move aside, unless you'd like to be charged with obstruction."

The attorney stepped aside, and the officer he'd spoken to leveled a fierce looking rifle at Fergus. The other policeman set about unlocking Fergus's chains. "Fergus McKay?" he said.

"Yes?"

"Hands on your head, please."

Fergus complied. The officer moved around behind Fergus, then snapped a handcuff around one wrist and directed it down behind Fergus's back. "You are being charged with second degree thought crime." The officer grasped the other wrist, directed it down toward the other, and snapped the other cuff around it. "Do you understand you are being charged with a crime?"

"I understand I'm being charged. What I don't understand is the charge."

"Take it up with the judge."

"What about my rights?"

"You can take that up with the judge, too."

The officer pushed Fergus toward the door. As he was hustled out of the room, Fergus turned to his attorney. "Option three!"

Randolph nodded as the room emptied. "It really is the best for all parties," he said to no one in particular. Then he retrieved his digipad from a pocket and called up his appointments. He shook his head. It was going to be a busy day. His schedule for the day was filled with half a dozen more consultations just like this one.

About the Author

Steve Coate writes and lives in sunny South Florida, where he struggles daily for dominion of the keyboard with his possessive tabby, Bigby. His short fiction has also appeared in *SNAFU: Wolves at the Door*, *Abbreviated Epics* from *Third Flatiron Anthologies* and *Plasma Frequency Magazine*. For a full bibliography, visit coaterack.blogspot.com. Follow Steve on Twitter @stevecoate for updates on his fiction. Readers can also drop him a line at stevecoate11@gmail.com.

*****~~~~~*****

Into the Light

by Paul Barclay

Years before the media began to call her contemporaries "The Hollow Generation," and mere months before hating her sprouted a hip cottage industry, Dr. Adelaide Lawrence stood in a high school gym under dim and flickering lights staring at her contraption. A black tripod as tall as her chest held an array of four glass orbs, looking like a very poor man's Christmas tree. She eyed the joint between the second and third globes and made an adjustment with her spanner.

She pulled on a pair of microfiber gloves and gingerly rotated the glass orbs around their small metal pegs. As she coaxed them into position, she worried about the reporter coming to interview her. She didn't know why she had agreed. It had been a brusque conversation in her usual style. Yes, this is Adelaide. Yes, I am in charge of Project ASTRAL. No, I cannot meet you for an interview. No time. When he suggested that he come visit her on the job, it seemed a simple solution. He would get his interview, and she would not have to take a break from her work. Still, it was only one reporter, and the project could use the exposure. Money was running out from her MacArthur Fellowship, and soon she would need to find investors.

The phone in her pocket buzzed, letting her know that it was too late for whatever trepidation she felt. That would be him texting from the parking lot. She settled the last orb and took a seat in the metal folding chair next to the device. She removed her phone from her pocket, texted to confirm that the doors to the gym were unlocked, and began answering emails from the hospital where she worked.

Six minutes later, Arnold Raider flung open the door to the gymnasium and strode across the paneled floor. The clacking of his bootheels bounced off the walls and chairs. "Dr. Lawrence, I presume." His voice boomed in the empty hall, and even he seemed surprised. "I'm Raider. We spoke on the phone. Hope I'm not interrupting." He tread between the multitude of folded chairs and took the seat directly next to Adelaide.

"No, it's fine. Good to see you made it," although she did not look up from her phone until she finished typing out an email to her department chair promising to keep him apprised of the night's proceedings. When she had, she slid her phone into her pocket and pulled a canvas bag from beneath her chair. "The event starts in an hour, which means we probably have about forty-five minutes before people begin arriving." She pulled a laptop from the bag and unfolded it across her lap.

"What sort of event is this? Seems like an odd location for a tech demo."

"This is not a tech demo, it's a pilot test. And in one hour this gym will be home to a small dance recital." She reached down to the base of the metal tripod and took hold of a thin black cable, which she connected to her laptop.

Raider chuckled. "Dance recital? You mean to tell me that this genius-grant-funded, future-of-all-communications technological marvel is going to be used to beam some guy in to watch the sixth-grade production of Swan Lake?" She frowned, and he leaned toward her and smiled. "I'm just joshing you. I don't mean anything by it. But, why here? Why this event?"

"She's five."

"Who?"

"The little girl who is dancing. She's five. This is her first performance, and she wanted her father to be here."

120

Raider slapped his knee. "Hah! See, it's even worse than I thought. Now you're using your techno-magic to enable some deadbeat dad that can't even be bothered to show up to his kid's dance recital. So, what's his excuse then? Power meeting in London?"

"Mr. Hughes is currently being treated for third degree burns covering eighty percent of his legs and fifty percent of his torso." In the silence that followed, each keystroke she made sounded like a hammerfall.

"Well. I guess that's a good excuse," Raider murmured.

"Yes. It is."

He fumbled with his notes, filling the tense quiet until he could manage to ask another question. "So, what got you started on this little adventure of yours, anyway?"

"Well, Mr. Raider, if I must pinpoint an origin, I'd say that Project ASTRAL began with the work of Dr. Hunter Hoffman." She looked up from the laptop and stared at him but saw no signs of recognition. "You should look him up. Amazing man. He built a virtual reality environment for burn patients called 'SnowWorld.' He had them play a little virtual reality game where they threw snowballs at penguins, while in the real world they were having their bandages changed or having the dead skin sloughed off of their burns. He found that with the pleasant distraction of the game, patients experienced much less pain. The effect rivaled that of opioid painkillers."

As she went on, her voice began to rise in pitch, and her sentences came faster. Where before she had spoken with one eye on the monitor, now she fixed her full attention on Raider. He leaned against the back of his chair, legs splayed wide in front of him.

"I worked in Hoffman's lab building virtual environments. He was a visionary. Always talking about how we can use games to reduce the pain and fear of real life. So that's where I got my start, even though I choose to focus on a different kind of pain. I mean, on the user end, ASTRAL is basically just a VR headset connected to a brainwave monitor."

"Now that's what I'm interested in," Raider said and leaned toward her. "What exactly does ASTRAL do, and how do you intend to put it to work?"

Adelaide waved her hand at the topmost glass orb. "This one is an omnidirectional camera. It streams video back to the lab computer, which converts it into an environment that can be viewed through a VR headset. Mr. Hughes is wearing that headset tonight, and he'll be able to look around, see everything that he would see if he was sitting here. That's the easy part. I perfected that years ago. People use that now for telecommuting and all sorts of mundane things.

"That was never enough for me, though. These other globes generate a hologram. It's currently programmed to create an image of Mr. Hughes before the accident. I modeled it after pictures his daughter showed me. That's also where the brainwave monitor comes in. You see, when you decide that you want to move, your brain generates this signal called a 'preresponse potential,' which. . . "

"Layman's terms, sweetheart," he leaned closer and patted her shoulder like a chiding grandmother, causing her to jerk slightly away. He didn't seem to notice. "I won't be able to understand the science of it, and neither will my readers. They only care about the human angle."

Adelaide sighed and looked down at her computer screen. People were starting to filter in and find seats for the recital. She checked the time, and when she saw that only ten minutes remained before showtime, a nervous pang shot through her gut.

"Suffice to say that you can use your brain to control the hologram. So, in addition to being able to turn his head and follow his daughter across the stage, the hologram's head will also turn. He should be able to move it in any way he could normally move his own body."

"But what about touch?" Raider chewed on his thumb and squinted at the device as though it might be the one to answer him. "I mean, holograms are made of light, correct? You can't slap it if it makes a rude remark, or give it a big friendly hug."

Adelaide rolled her eyes. "There is a multitude of people in this world that you can't hug, Mr. Raider."

"Fair enough, Ms. Lawrence. But your project website talks about a future where this sort of thing becomes common. Don't you think that something like that would enable a world where people are even more disconnected than they are today? Imagine going to a football game with your friends, but they were too busy to leave the house, so now you're in the bleachers with a couple of holograms instead. Or even a scenario like this one, but with a father who doesn't have a medical excuse, he's just a workaholic or doesn't care."

The room had grown quite full by now, and several people were listening to them talk. Adelaide felt her face grow warm, and when she responded she nearly hissed. "Planes drop bombs, Mr. Raider, but they also carry sick people to hospitals and distant relatives to their weddings. There are people who misuse them, yes, but you do not attribute their pathologies to Orville Wright."

"So, are you saying that the good outweighs the bad, or are you just saying that it's not your responsibility to care?"

Before Adelaide could answer, the lights dimmed in the gymnasium. A balding man in an oversized and overworn blazer announced that the recital was about to begin, and would everyone please be quiet. After a few rapid taps at her laptop keyboard, she leaned toward Raider and whispered, "Here we go." She flipped a switch on the central shaft of the tripod next to her, and there was a faint hum, then silence. After a few seconds, a dim sheath of light enveloped the device, at first translucent but growing more opaque by the second.

When Adelaide reached into the veil of light and made a small twisting motion, the sheath of light resolved into the figure of a man. He glowed only a little, his deep brown face and arms held only the slightest trace of golden light. The figure held preternaturally still for a few moments, until the eyes began to blink. "Very good, Mr. Hughes. Can you see me?"

The hologram turned its head, first right, then left, to find her. When it did, a profoundly human smile spread across its face. "Dr. L! I can see you! I'm there!" Mr. Hughes' projection began to shift around in its chair, and raised its hands to its face. "I thought I was lighter than that, Dr. L.," he said and grinned.

"I adjusted your skin tone to be a bit darker, Mr. Hughes. Since the lights were going to be dim here, I didn't want your glow to be too disruptive for the other parents. I know it's not accurate. . . "

"No, no, it's wonderful! It's better than wonderful," he cut her off. "I barely remember what my arms looked like before, anyways." He beamed as steadily as though the image of his face had frozen that way.

"I'm glad you're happy with it. Another bit of good news is that Opal's part of the first group going on, so you won't miss your bedtime. Just let me know if you can see the stage clearly."

Mr. Hughes' nodded. "Thanks Dr. L. This means the world to me. To Opal, too."

Arnold Raider's mouth had fallen ajar, but he closed it and jotted some notes. He whispered, a slight quiver in his voice. "It is alright if I touch?"

"Do you mind, Mr. Hughes?" she asked, still facing the projection. When Mr. Hughes gave assent, she responded, "Stay near the exterior, Mr. Raider. I don't want you knocking about the projectors."

124

Raider rose from his chair and kneeled in front of the hologram, extending his hand. A gentle heat radiated from its surface like remnants of a campfire. His hand snapped away as soon as it made contact, and he shivered noticeably. "I'll give you one thing. It's more lifelike than I imagined."

Adelaide might have responded, but before she could the house lights fell. She settled into her seat, and Raider scuttled by and climbed into his, as the first tinkling notes of Clair de Lune began. A row of small girls in pink slippers and leotards shuffled onto the stage, each painted about the eyes with feathery eyeliner. The girl bringing up the rear had darker skin than the rest, almost a burnt caramel, and she had her father's dimples.

As the piano lilted through the rote strains of the song, each girl circled to the front of the stage and turned or leapt or spun as they had been taught, the others moving rhythmically behind. As the piece entered its fifth minute, it was Opal's turn to take her solo. Unlike the others, she moved with a natural fluidity. She bounced and slid across the floor and raised her hands above her head and spun, eyes locked straight forward, until her head whipped around with the spin and turned front once again. She seemed out of place among the other five year olds, like an older soul inhabited her body while she moved and guided her limbs according to some polished and classical ambition. But when the song was done and bows were had, she couldn't restrain herself any longer. Opal broke from her group and ran toward her father's radiant image.

"Daddy, did you see me?" she said and dropped to her knees beside him.

"Baby, you were beautiful," he choked, and a golden tear slid down his cheek. He leaned toward her and took her face in his hands and kissed her head like he had done every night before his accident. His hands passed through her a bit, and the kiss landed somewhere beneath her forehead, but she closed her eyes and giggled.

"Daddy, it's warm." She scooted forward into the hologram until Adelaide was concerned that she might knock over the tripod, and wriggled as the warm light flashed across her skin, distorting the image. She stayed nestled inside the hollow of his form as other parents gawked, many expressing appreciation and many others with disgust, until the next dancers took the stage and began their own undulations. Opal fell asleep with her head against Adelaide's calf.

After the show, Raider looked on as Mr. Hughes said goodbye to his daughter and told her that her aunt and uncle would bring her to see him tomorrow. They attempted a hug, but Opal squeezed too much, and her arm touched one of the white-hot globes on the machine. She yelped and jumped back, but seemed otherwise unaffected. When Opal had left with her aunt, Adelaide bid Mr. Hughes goodnight and turned off the machine.

Raider stood and folded up his papers, shoving them into his coat pocket. "I think I have everything I need. I'll get you a proof of the article before it goes out. Probably two weeks. Unless you want to get together for dinner some time and talk about it then."

"I eat all of my dinners on the job, Mr. Raider," Adelaide replied, and as if to illustrate she reached into her bag and produced a sandwich sealed in a plastic bag. She did not look at him, but waved the sandwich dismissively.

"Alright then," he shuffled backward a little, and when she did not look up, he called out a farewell. "Good night, Adelaide. I don't fully understand what you've got here, but it's truly something else."

"Good night Mr. Raider," she echoed, and said nothing else.

..""

Into the Light

Two weeks later, after many thanks from the Hughes family and many adoring hugs from Opal Hughes in particular, Adelaide Lawrence sat by herself in her office wearing a microfiber glove and holding one of the glass spheres from the Project ASTRAL device in her hand. Her laptop was open to an article in the *Journal of Electrical Energy and Technology,* entitled "A Comparative Study of Heat Dispersal Optimization for Convex Lenses."

She heard the familiar plunk from her computer that indicated new email. Glancing at it from the corner of her eye, she saw that it was from Mr. Raider. Her stomach dropped inside her gut, and she set the glass orb down gingerly on the desk. She had fretted about the article for the last two weeks and knew that she wouldn't be able to concentrate until she read it.

The body of the email was terse and apologetic. "Sorry. The article is a bit harsh. You seem like a sweetheart, but editor says this is punchier. This is the final version. —R."

Adelaide read the title of the article and stopped there. She felt a strong urge to fling the laptop across the room. After a few moments, her fists unclenched, and she closed the email. She folded her laptop and put it away, as though to distance herself from the whole ordeal. But she could not prise the title from her head. "You Can't Hug a Hologram."

Raider's editor was right. It stuck with you. She repeated it in her head several times before the buzzing sensation in her gut subsided and her heart stopped pounding.

Adelaide turned to the bauble on her desk that represented her work for the last five years and stared at its shimmering surface. "I guess it's true. You can't," she muttered to herself and rested her head in her hands, as she did when she was deep in thought. Then she looked up, and her eyes glittered as though they were made of the same glass as her device. She spoke again to herself, but now her defeat was replaced with something sterner, something sharper.

"You can't," she repeated. "Yet." And then she went back to work.

About the Author

Paul Barclay hails from Houston, Texas, where he has lived for ten years. He currently works in a research hospital studying smoking cessation. In his spare time he loves to read, write, play video games, and ride his bicycle.

*****~~~~~*****

Credits and Acknowledgments

Illustrations

Cover image and design – Keely Rew

Ebook Only:
Super Bugs - Red blood cells on an agar plate used to diagnose bacterial infection. Wikimedia Commons, uploaded by National Cancer Institute.

Carnival of Colours – Holi Festival, Spanish Fork, Utah - Sri Sri Radha Lotus Temple, author Steven Gerner, commons.wikimedia.org

Killing the Tree Spirit – Jack Frost battles with the Green man – commons.wikimedia.org. Uploaded to Flickr by user Ranveig

Into the Light – The Dance Class, Edgar Degas (1874), Musee d'Orsay. Commons.wikimedia.org, transferred by User: Ireas

Readers

Andrew Cairns, Tom Parker, Keely Rew

Discover other titles by Third Flatiron:

(1) Over the Brink: Tales of Environmental Disaster

(2) A High Shrill Thump: War Stories

(3) Origins: Colliding Causalities

(4) Universe Horribilis

(5) Playing with Fire

(6) Lost Worlds, Retraced

(7) Redshifted: Martian Stories

(8) Astronomical Odds

(9) Master Minds

(10) Abbreviated Epics

(11) The Time It Happened

www.thirdflatiron.com

THIRD FLATIRON